Stories, History, Traditions,

Music and Humour

of

the Highland Bagpipe

TUNES
OF GLORY

By
W. L. Manson

TUNES
OF GLORY

Tunes of Glory is a condensed and edited edition of "The Highland Bagpipe" by W. L. Manson, which was first published in 1901 by Alexander Gardner of Paisley and London.

This edition published by Lang Syne Publishers Ltd, 45 Finnieston Street, Glasgow, in November 1992, and printed by Dave Barr Print, Glasgow.

ISBN No. 1 85217 002 6

ORIGINS OF THE PIPES

Without the bag the pipe is the most ancient of all instruments. Boys on their way to school pulled a green straw from the cornfield, bit off a bit, trimmed the end and had a ready made pipe. It was quite natural that people should try to form sounds by blowing through a tube, and afterwards to vary the sounds either by varying the size or shape of the tube or by fitting into it some special mechanism.

The pipe was well known to the Trojans, Egyptians, Greeks, and Romans, who had different kinds for different measures, and from contemporary writings we learn that the strain of blowing these early pipes was so great that the player had to bandage his lips and cheeks with a leathern muzzle.

One ancient picture represents a player blowing a triple pipe, that is, three pipes joined at the mouth-piece, but separate further down, a performance which must have made the need for some improved method of supplying wind very obvious.

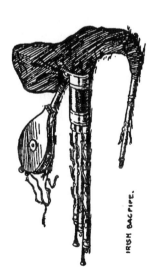

IRISH BAGPIPE.

MacLean, in his *History of the Celtic Language*, considers the bagpipe as originally consisting of a bladder with drones and chanter of reeds and bulrushes, and affirms that he himself made and played on such an instrument.

The first real bagpipe would, however, be a skin, most likely that of a goat or kid, and the invention of the valve in the mouth piece would follow as a matter of course - that is, if the man who thought of the bag did not also think of having a bellows.

There were no drones in the early pipes. St. Jerome, who lived in the fifth century, says that at the synagogue, in ancient times there was a simple species of bagpipe, consisting of a skin or leather bag, with two pipes, through one of which the bag was inflated, the other emitting the sound. This was the first real bagpipe and it was also, it may be added, the germ of the organ, for the bagpipe is the organ reduced to its simplest expression.

At the opening of the 20th century there were three recognised kinds of bagpipes in Britain:-

1. The Northumbrian bagpipe.
2. The Irish bagpipe
3. The Great Highland bagpipe.

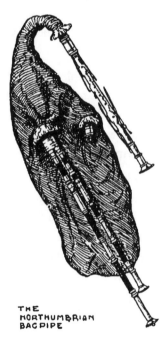

THE
NORTHUMBRIAN
BAGPIPE

The Northumbrian bagpipe is in two forms, one like the Highland, but of smaller dimensions and a milder tone, and the other a miniature of this, and having the same relation to it as the fife has to a German band. The Lowland bagpipe of Scotland may be identified with the Northumbrian, but it is looked on rather contemptuously by the devotees of the Highland, because, in their opinion, it merely imitates other instruments, and is not fitted to perform what they consider the perfection of pipe music - the pibroch.

The Northumbrian and Lowland pipes were easily carried about, and were much gentler than the great Highland, but did not resemble those used on the Continent. They had the same tone as the Highland, but were less sonorous, and were blown by a bellows put in motion by the arm opposite to that under which the bag was held. In this latter respect they were similar to the Irish, and like them they had the drones fixed in one stock and laid horizontally over the arm, not borne on the shoulder. The real Lowland bagpipe, however, never got farther than two drones.

The Irish bagpipe is the instrument in its most elaborate form. It also is supplied with wind by a bellows. The drones are all fixed on one stock, and have keys which are played by the wrist of the right hand. The reeds are soft and the tones very sweet and melodious, and there is a harmonious bass which is very effective in the hands of a good player. Some of the drones are of great length, winding as many as three times the length of the apparent tube. The player is seated with one side of the bellows tied firmly to his body, the other to his right arm, the drones under his left leg, and the end of the chanter resting on a pad of leather on his knee, on which it is tipped for the purpose of articulating many of the notes. The bag is made of goat's skin and is rendered pliable by means of bees' wax and butter. Originally it, like that of the Highland pipe, was filled by the mouth, but it was changed so as to be filled by the bellows. In later instruments several finger keys were adapted to a fourth tube, whereby a perfect chord could be produced, and thus the instrument was rendered fit for private apartments, whereas the Highland and the Lowland were only suitable for the open air.

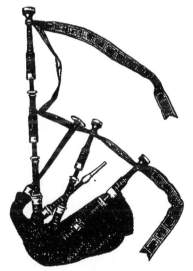

THE GREAT HIGHLAND BAGPIPE

And lastly, we have the "Great Highland Bagpipe." In this instrument a valved tube leads from the mouth to an air-tight bag which has four other orifices, three large enough to contain the base of three fixed long tubes termed drones, and another smaller, to which is fitted the chanter. The three are thrown on the shoulder while the latter is held in the hands. All four pipes are fitted with reeds, but of different kinds. The drone reeds are made by splitting a round length of "cane" or reed backward from a cross cut near a knot or joint towards the open end. They thus somewhat resemble the reed in organ pipes, the loose flap of cane replacing the tongue, and the uncut part the tube or reed proper. They are set downward in a chamber at the base of the drone, so that the current of air issuing from the bag tends to set the tongue in vibration. The drone reeds are only intended to produce a single note, which can be tuned by a "slider" on the pipe itself, varying the length of the consonating air column.

The chanter reed is different in form, being made of two approximated edges of cane tied on to a metal tube. It is thus essentially a double reed, like that of the oboe or bassoon, while the drone reed roughly represents the single beating reed of the organ or clarinet. The drone reed is an exact reproduction of the "squeaker" which children in the fields fashion out of joints of tall grass, probably the oldest form of this reed in existence.

The drones are in length proportional to their note, the longest being about three feet high. The chanter is a conical wooden tube, about fourteen inches long, pierced with eight sounding holes, seven in front for the fingers and one at the top behind for the thumb of the left hand. Two additional holes bored across the tube below the lowest of these merely regulate the pitch, and are never stopped; were it not for them, however, the chanter would require to be some inches shorter, and would consequently have a less pleasing appearance.

The two smaller drones produce a note in unison with the lowest A of the chanter, and the larger an octave lower. The indescribable thrill which the bagpipe is capable of imparting is produced by a sudden movement of the fingers on certain notes, which gives an expression peculiar to the pipes, and distinguishes the pibroch from all other music. The drones, as has been said, are tuned by means of "sliders" or movable joints, and this tuning, or preparation for playing, which generally occupies a few minutes of the piper's time before he begins the tune proper, is heard with impatience by those not accustomed to the instrument.

The Highland bagpipe is louder and more shrill that any other, probably because it was all along intended for use as an instrument of war, and pipe music is known to have been heard at a distance of six miles, and, under specially favourable circumstances, of ten miles. The Duke of Sutherland has a bagpipe which was played on in the '45, and could be heard at a distance of eight miles.

Modern pipes are generally made of black ebony or cocoa-wood, the ferrules or rings being of ivory. Sometimes the pipes are half-mounted in silver, that is the high ferrules in ivory and the low in silver. The drones of the best makers have the inside lined with metal, where there is friction in the tuning slide. The bag is formed of sheepskin, in which are securely fastened five pieces of turned wood called stocks. These receive the ends of the chanter, the mouth-piece, and the drones. The chanter reed is formed of two pieces of Spanish cane, placed side by side. The tops of these are worked down to a fine edge, and the bottoms are tied with fine hemp to a small metal tube. The blow-pipe has on its lower end a valve, which prevents the return of the wind to the mouth. The drones provide a background or additional volume of sound, which gives body to the music. The big drone is fitted with two, and the others with one tuning slide each. The drones are interchangeable, so that the big drone can be placed in the right or left stock to suit a right or left-handed player. When the bag is filled with wind the pressure of the player's arm must be so regulated that there is always just sufficient force of air to bring out the notes clearly without interfering with the steady action of the drones. The bag is held well under the arm, the big drone rests on the shoulders, and the others are suspended from it by ribbons and silk cords. The bag is generally held slightly in front, so that the short drones rest on the shoulder. When on full-dress parade a banner flies from the big drone, with the arms of the regiment or chief as a motto. The drones are generally placed on the left shoulder, but many players place them on the right. The whole instrument is kept in position by the tension of the bag.

FROM HARP TO PIPES

The harp was the immediate predecessor of the pipes; but in ancient times, and also contemporary with the harp, there were other instruments. The *Complaynt of Scotland*, written in 1548, speaking of a company of musicians, says:-

"The fyrst hed ane drone bagpipe, the next hed ane pipe made of ane bleddir and of ane reid, the third playit on ane trump, the feyerd on ane cornepipe, the fyfth playit on ane pipe made of ane grait horne, the sext playit on ane recorder, the sevint plait on ane fiddil, and the last on ane quhissel."

We cannot speak as to quality, but there was evidently no lack of quantity in these days.

The *Horn of Battle* was used by the ancient Caledonians to call their armies together. The *cornu* was blown by the Druids and their Christian successors, and St. Patrick is represented as carrying one. Ancient writers, indeed, lay particular stress on the musical ability of the Celtic

HARPER: ON A STONE AT MONIFEITH
From *Chalmers' Sculptured Stones of Scotland.*

priesthood, the members of which they describe as possessing extraordinary skill as harpers, taking prominent part with their instruments in religious ceremonies. The *cornu* in its rudest form was a cow's horn, and could sometimes be heard at a distance of six miles. The Irish Celts had various other instruments, but the harp was the favourite, both in Scotland and Ireland.

The transition from the harp to the bagpipe was spread over about two centuries. In 1565 George Buchanan speaks of the Highlanders using both instruments, and during the seventeenth century the uses of the harp declined to such an extent that the number of professional harpers was very small indeed. The civil wars largely accounted for this, as the fitness of the bagpipe for the tumult of battle gave it an easy superiority over the harp.

When the pipes became paramount is about as difficult to determine as when they first threatened the position of the harp. They seem to have existed alongside the harp and the coronach and the fiery cross for a considerable time, as we have references to all these in the literature of the sixteenth and seventeenth and eighteenth centuries. John MacLeod of Dunvegan, who lived about 1650, had a harper, a piper, and a fool, all of whom were most liberally provided for. We have got a blind harper, *Ruaraidh Dall*, harper to MacLeod of Glenelg, and a blind piper, *Ian Dall*, piper to MacKenzie of Gairloch, each of whom excelled in his own sphere, and both of whom flourished about 1650.

DIARY OF THE BAGPIPES

That the bagpipe is an instrument of great antiquity is an admitted fact, but whether it is one of those referred to in Scripture is another matter. The pipe without the bag is mentioned in I Sam. x. 5, Isaiah v. 12, and Jer. xiviii, 36, but the pipe without the bag is not the bagpipe. There have been many attempts made to identify the instrument with one or other of those named in Scripture, and in histories of Scripture times, but these are all based on conjecture. An instrument is mentioned which was composed of two reeds perforated according to rule, and united to a leathern bag, called in Persian *nie amban*; and in Egypt a similar instrument is described as consisting of two flutes, partly of wood and partly of iron. Another traveller tells of an Arabian instrument which consisted of a double chanter with several apertures, and in 1818 ancient engravings were found in the northern states of Africa which seemed to prove that an instrument like the bagpipe had existed in Scripture times. The Chaldeans and Babylonians had two peculiar instruments, the *Sambuka* and the *Symphonia*, and some historians identify the latter as the *sackbut*, the alleged ancestor of the bagpipe. Others assert that a form of the bagpipe was used in the services of the Temple at Jerusalem, but this in any case, may be treated as the merest of conjecture.

The historical references to the instrument as having existed at all in these days are few and far between:-

385 B.C. - Theocritus, a writer who flourished about this date, mentions it incidentally in his pastorals, but not in such a way as to give any indication of what form it assumed.

200 B.C. - An ancient terra cotta excavated at Tarsus by Mr. W. Burchhardt, and supposed to date from 200 B.C., represents a piper with a wind instrument with vertical rows of reed pipes, firmly attached to him. The instrument has also been found sculptured in ancient Nineveh.

A.D. 1. - There is a singular tradition in the Roman Catholic Church to the effect that the shepherds who first saw the infant Messiah in the stable expressed their gladness by playing on the bagpipe. This is, of course, possible, but there is only the tradition and the likelihood that the shepherds would have musical instruments of some kind to support the theory. Albrecht Durer, a famous German artist of the 16th century, has perpetuated the idea in a woodcut of the Nativity, in which he represents one of the shepherds playing on the pipes, but his work is, naturally, founded on the tradition. The illuminator of a Dutch missal in the library of King's College, Aberdeen, has taken liberties with the tradition and given the bagpipe to one of the appearing angels, who uses it for playing a salute.

A.D. 54. - The cruel Emperor Nero was an accomplished musician, and a contorniate of his time has given rise to many assertions connecting him with the pipes. It is generally referred to as a coin, but it is in reality a contorniate or medal, which was given away at public sports. The sketch here reproduced (full-size) is from a specimen in the British Museum, and very little study will show that it proves almost nothing

REPRODUCED FROM A CONTORNIATE IN THE BRITISH MUSEUM.

relating to the bagpipe. The obverse bears the head of Nero and the usual inscription. On the reverse there seems to be the form of a wind organ with nine irregular pipes, all blown by a bellows and having underneath what is probably a bag. It is more closely related to the organ than to the bagpipe, and, as has been said, it proves nothing. Some writers call the instrument on which Nero played a flute with a bladder under the performer's arm, a description which does more to identify it as the bagpipe. It cannot have been considered a very honourable thing in Nero's day to play the pipes, for the emperor on hearing of the last revolt, that which cost him his throne and his life, vowed solemnly that if the gods would but extricate him from his troubles he would play in public on the bagpipe, as a sort of penance or thank offering probably. Perhaps history has made a mistake, and it may have been the pipes and not the fiddle Nero played on while Rome was burning. The medal, it may be added, is believed by the authorities at the British Museum to date from about A.D. 330, although it bears the impress of Nero.

That the instrument was in use among the Romans is indisputable. A historian, who wrote a history of the wars of the Persians, the Vandals, and the Goths, states that the Roman infantry used it for marching purposes, and he describes it as having both skin and wood extremely fine. The name it went by was *pythaula*, a word of Greek origin which bears a striking resemblance to the Celtic *piob-mhala*, pronounced *piovala*. There is in Rome a fine Greek sculpture in *basso relievo* representing a piper playing on an instrument closely resembling the Highland bagpipe, the performer himself being dressed not unlike a modern Highlander. It is shown besides on several coins, but from the rudeness of the drawings or their decay the exact form cannot be ascertained.

About 1870 a stone was dug from the ground near Bo'ness, on which was sculptured a party of Roman soldiers on the march. They were dressed in short kilts, and one was playing the bagpipe. The instrument was very similar to those of the present day except that the drones were shorter.

A.D.100 - Aristides Quintilianus, who lived about this time, writes to the effect that the bagpipe was known in the Scottish Highlands in his day. This, however, may be set aside as a reference of no value seeing that the Highlands was then an unknown world to the Greeks. The Greeks of the same age knew the instrument as *Tibia utricularis*, and from the pipes, we are told, the Athenian shepherds drew the sweetest sounds. Other books again tell us that the Athenians rejected the pipes because they disturbed conversation and made hearing difficult. Still others - English be it noted - contain the sentence, "Arcadia in Greece: the bagpipe was first invented here," but the statement is not substantiated in any way.

A.D. 500 - In the sixth century the bagpipe is mentioned by Procopius, a Greek historian, as the instrument of the Roman infantry, the trumpet being that of the cavalry.

A.D. 800 - There is a picture of a primitive instrument copied from a manuscript of the ninth century. It consists of a blow pipe on one side of a small bag, with a sort of chanter having three or four holes and a beast's head instead of the usual bell-shaped end. The instrument was held extended from the mouth, and the bag, if any pressure was necessary, must have been elastic, as it could not be pressed in any way.

A.D. 1118 - Giraldus Cambrensis, the historian, mentions the pipes about this date as Welsh and Irish, but not as Scottish. But *The Complaynt of Scotland*, written in 1548, states that the instrument was a favourite with the Scottish peasantry "from the earliest periods". Another trustworthy record says it was in use in Scotland and Wales about the end of the twelfth century. Besides, Pennant in his *Tour* was told that it was mentioned in the oldest northern songs as the "soeck-pipe." There is little doubt it was cultivated to some extent in Scotland in the twelfth century.

A.D. 1136 - In Melrose Abbey, built in 1136, there were two carvings representing bagpipes, but they are not supposed to be of a date so early as the abbey itself. The first, that of an aged musician, is given in Sir John Graham Dalziel's *Musical Memoirs of Scotland*, published in 1849. It is a gargoyle in the form of a pig carrying a rude bagpipe under its head with the drone, the only pipe now remaining, on its left shoulder, and its fore feet, what is left of them, clasped around the bag. The mouth is open and the rain water off the roof runs through it. There is a tradition that as James IV was not very well regarded by Highlanders the pig playing their favourite instrument was placed in the abbey as a satire. The chapel, however, on the outside of the nave of which the carving is, was built before the time of James IV. It is curious that all, or nearly all, the carvings on the outside of the abbey are ugly, some of them gruesome, while the figures on the inside are beautiful. This, it is supposed, was meant to convey the idea of Heaven inside and earth outside. In the architecture of the middle ages the gargoyle, or waterspout, assumed a vast variety of forms, often frightful, fantastic or grotesque. So the carving in Melrose Abbey may be simply the product of the artist's imagination. Besides, a French architect had a good deal to do with the abbey, so the designs may not all be emblematic of Scottish life of the date when they were made. In *Musical Memoirs of Scotland* it is stated that the instrument had two drones, one on each side of the animal's head, and a chanter which hung beneath its feet, these latter being placed on the apertures. The figure seems to have been very much worn away since this book was written.

A.D. 1200 - Coming down to ages of which we have better historical records, we find a drawing of the thirteenth century which shows a girl dancing on the shoulders of a jester to the music of the instrument in its simplest form, the chanter only.

A.D. 1300 - About the end of the thirteenth century the bagpipe in France was consigned to the lower orders, and only used by the blind and the wandering or mendicant classes. Polite society, however, resumed it in the time of Louis XIV and Louis XV.

A.D. 1307 - Several payments to performers of the fourteenth and subsequent centuries are recorded. In the reign of Edward II there is a payment to *Jauno Chevretter* (the latter word meant bagpiper) for playing before the king.

A.D. 1314 - The Clan Menzies are alleged to have had their pipes with them at Bannockburn, and they are supposed to have been played by one of the MacIntyres, their hereditary pipers. The Clan Menzies claim that these pipes are still in existence, at least three portions of them, - the chanter, which has the same number of finger holes as the modern chanter, but two additional holes on each side; the blowpipe, which is square, but graduates to round at the top; and the drone, of which the top half only remains. These relics, which are now preserved with great care, are supposed to be the remains of a set which were played to the clan when they mustered at Castle Menzies, and marched to join the main body of the Scottish army at Torwood, and in front of them on the field of battle. There are said to be MacDonald pipes in existence, which consist of a chanter and blowpipe only, and which, it is alleged, were played before the Macdonalds at Bannockburn. This, most likely, also refers to the Menzies pipes, as the MacIntyres, who are credited with having been owners of each, were at different times pipers to the Menzies and to the Clan Ranald branch of the MacDonalds. Bruce's son, says another tradition, had pipes at Bannockburn. Sir Walter Scott represents the men of the Isles as charging to the sound of the bagpipe; and David MacDonald, a Clan MacDonald bard, who wrote about 1838, in a poem on the battle, says that when the bards began to encourage the clans, the pipers began to blow their pipes. There is, however, no historical proof that the instrument was used at the battle. Though horns and trumpets are mentioned by reliable historians, it is not till about two hundred years later that the bagpipe is referred to as having superseded the trumpet as an instrument of war.

A.D. 1327 - In the reign of Edward III two pipers received permission to visit schools for minstrels beyond the seas, and from about that time till the sixteenth century the bagpipe was the favourite instrument of the Irish kerns.

A.D. 1362 - There is an entry in the Exchequer rolls of 1362 of forty shillings "paid to the King's pipers", which indicates the use of the pipes at that date.

A.D. 1370 - The arms of Winchester School, founded in 1370, show an angel playing a bagpipe, and a silver-mounted crosier, presented by the founder to the New College, Oxford, has among other figures that of an angel playing the bagpipe. Some enthusiast might surely have adduced the frequent connections of the instrument with angels as proof of its sacred origin.

A.D. 1377 - One "claryoner," two trumpeters and four pipers were attached to the fleet of Richard, Earl of Arundel (Richard II). The bagpipe often appears in the English sculpture of the fourteenth and fifteenth centuries, and, of course, very frequently later.

A.D. 1380 - There are no English literary references to the pipes till the time of Chaucer, when the poet makes the miller in the *Canterbury Tales* play on the instrument:-

"A baggepipe wel cowde he blowe and sowne,
And therewithal he broughte us out of towne."

So it seems that the company of pilgrims left London, accompanied by the strains of the bagpipe. It must have been in fairly general use, else the poet would not have worked it into his composition, but there are no means of discovering how long before this it had been in favour in England.

A.D. 1390 - At the battle between the clans Quhale and Chattan on the North Inch of Perth, Rev. James MacKenzie tells us in his *History of Scotland*, which is generally accepted as authoritative, the clans "stalked into the barriers to the sound of their own great war pipes."

A.D. 1400 - The bagpipe is supposed to have been first used officially in war in Britain at the beginning of the fifteenth century.

Lowland Piper   Highland Piper   Irish Piper

A.D. 1406-37 - James I of Scotland played on the "chorus", a word in which some interpret as meaning the bagpipe. Besides we are also told that he played on "the tabour, the bagpipes, the organ, the flute, the harp, the trumpet, and the shepherd's reed." He must have been a versatile monarch. If he really wrote *Peblis to the Play*, the fact proves that if he did not play the pipes he was quite familiar with their existence, for he says:-

"With that Will Swane came smeitant out,
Ane meikle miller man,
Gif I sall dance have done, lat se
Blow up the bagpype than."

And also in another place:-
"The bag pipe blew and they outhrew
Out of the townis untald."

Except that he gives us the first really authentic historical Scottish reference to the pipes, King James and his connection with the music is rather a puzzling subject.

A.D. 1409 - What is believed to be the oldest authentic specimen of the bagpipe now existing is that in the possession of Messrs. J. & R. Glen, of Edinburgh, which bears the date 1409. Except that it wants the large drone, which was added at the beginning of the eighteenth century, it is very much the Highland pipe of the present day. The following is a description of the instrument:-

"Highland bagpipe, having two small drones and chanter, finely ornamented with Celtic patterns carved in circular bands. The drones are inserted in a stock apparently formed from a forked branch, the fork giving the drones their proper spread for the shoulder. In the centre of the stock are the letters 'R. McD,' below them a galley, and below the galley is the date in Roman numerals, M:CCCC:IX. The letters both in the initials above the galley and in the numeral inscription are of the Gothic form commonly used in the fifteenth century. On the reverse of the stock is a triplet of foliageous scroll work. Bands of interlaced work encircle the ends of the forked part, which are bound with brass ferrules. The lower joint of one of the drones is ornamented with a band of interlaced work in the centre. The corresponding joint of the other drone is not original. The upper joints of the drones are ornamented at both extremities with interlaced work and the finger holes, seven in number,

are greatly worn. The nail heads placed round the lower part of the bell of the chanter are decorated with engraved ornament. The bag and blowpipe are modern."

THE OLDEST EXISTING PIPES

It should be added that very little is known of the story of this old bagpipe, and the date carved on the stock is all that justifies us in attributing it to the fifteenth century. Also that its claims to antiquity are disputed by an instrument in the possession of the Duke of Sutherland, which is said to have been played at the battle of Sheriffmuir.

A.D. 1411 - We have the statement of Rev. James MacKenzie that at the Battle of Harlaw the Highland host came down "with pibrochs deafening to hear." Mr. MacKenzie, however, wrote at quite a recent date, and it would be interesting to know his authority. We do know, of course, that what is now a pipe tune was played at Harlaw, but that in itself proves nothing, since the earliest known copy of the music is not arranged for the pipes.

A.D. 1419 - An inventory of the instruments in St. James's Palace, made in 1419, specifies "four bagpipes with pipes of ivorie," and another "baggepipe with pipes of ivorie, the bagge covered with purple vellat."

A.D. 1430 - From this time on till the Reformation the bagpipe was fairly popular in the Lowlands of Scotland, and it is most likely that its use became general in the Highlands about 1500.

A.D. 1431 - At the battle of Inverlochy in 1431, we are told the pipes were played. This may have been supposed from the fact that we have a pipe tune of that date, but it is probable enough.

A.D. 1440 - In Rosslyn Chapel, Midlothian, built in 1440, there are two figures represented as playing the pipes. The first, an angelic piper, is of a class of which specimens are to be found in various sacred edifices throughout England. It is in the Lady Chapel, and is not therefore much noticed by visitors. The other figure is one of a pair which are carved as if they were supporting one end of one of the arches of the roof. What meaning they were supposed to convey it is impossible now to determine, but the representation of the piper is obvious enough.

A.D. 1485-1509 - In Henry VII's Chapel at Westminster there is a grotesque carving representing a bagpipe. Similar carvings appear at Hull, Great Yarmouth, Beverley, and Boston.

A.D. 1489 - In July, 1489, we find there was a payment of £8.8s. to "Inglish pyparis that com to the Castel (Edinburgh) and playit to the king;" and in 1505 another to "Inglis Pipar with the drone." So the instrument must have been as much English as Scottish at that time.

A.D. 1491 - Here again we find the "Inglis" piper to the front. In August of this year a party of them received seven unicorns, that is gold coins, at Linlithgow for playing to the king. Both of these payments are recorded in the accounts of the treasurer of the Royal household.

CARVINGS IN ROSSLYN CHAPEL

A.D. 1494 - In the ninth year of Henry VII there was paid to "Pudsey, piper on the bagpipes," 6s.8d. (approx. 33p).

A.D. 1500 - At a sale of curios in London in the summer of 1899 a jug was disposed of on which there was a painting of a mule playing a bagpipe. The article fetched £200, but it cannot be proved that the painting dates from the sixteenth century, though that is the certified date of the jug. About this time the second drone was added.

A.D. 1506 - 1582 - George Buchanan is the first to mention the bagpipe in connection with Gaelic-speaking people, and when he does mention it, it is solely as a military instrument. The harp was still the domestic musical instrument.

A.D. 1509 - 1547 - We have a curious set of wood-cuts of the time of Henry VIII one of which represents a piper dancing to the *Dance of Death* clothed according to the fashion of that time. He is dancing with a jester, who has the tonsure of a monk and wears a sort of kilt. We also know of a suit of armour made for Henry VIII on which the figure of a piper is engraved.

A.D. 1513 - It is on record that John Hastie, the celebrated hereditary piper of Jedburgh, played at the battle of Flodden. There is a painting of this date by the German artist, Albrecht Durer, which represents a

GERMAN PIPER OF THE SIXTEENTH CENTURY
From the Painting by Albrecht Durer.

shepherd boy playing to his sheep on the bagpipe, and another which shows a piper leaning against a tree with a naked dirk at the left side and a purse exactly like the sporran suspended in front. Olaus Magnus, a Swedish prelate of the same century, affirms that a double pipe, probably the bagpipe, was carried by the shepherds to the pastures that their flocks might feed better.

A.D. 1529 - At a procession in Brussels in 1529 in honour of the Virgin Mary, "many wild beasts danced round a cage containing two apes playing on the bagpipes." This statement may be taken for what it is worth. It is difficult to construct a theory that will explain it.

A.D. 1536 - In this year the bagpipe was played at church service in Edinburgh.

A.D. 1547 - 1553 - Among the musicians of Edward VI at the Court of England was "Richard Woodward, bagpiper," who had a salary of £12, not a princely sum. An entertainment was got up at court in this reign, part of which was a "maske of bagpypes."

A.D. 1548 - Among the eight musical instruments mentioned in *The Complaynt of Scotland*, written in 1548, there are included "ane drone bagpipe" and "ane pipe made one ane bleddir and of ane reid."

A.D. 1549 - A French officer describing warfare near Edinburgh in 1549, says "The wild Scots encouraged themselves to arms by the sounds of their bagpipes."

A.D. 1556 - The Queen Regent of Scotland headed a procession in honour of St. Giles, the patron saint of Edinburgh, and she was "accompanied by bagpipers and other musicians."

A.D. 1570 - Three St. Andrews pipers were admonished not to play on Sundays or at nights.

A.D. 1581 - We find James VI returning from church at Dalkeith one Sunday with two pipers playing before him; and, strangely enough, a little nearer the end of the century, we read, two pipers were prosecuted for playing on the Sunday. At various times between 1591 and 1596 pipers from the Water of Leith bound themselves strictly not to play on the Sundays. There was evidently one law for the king and another for the subject.

A.D. 1594 - At the Battle of Balrinnes, a witch who accompanied the Earl of Argyll referred in a prediction to the bagpipe as the principal military instrument of the Scottish mountaineers.

A.D. 1598 - An unpublished poem by Rev. Alex. Hume, minister of Logie, about 1598, contains the lines:-

"Caus michtilie the warlie nottes brake
On Heiland pipes, Scottes and Hyberniche."

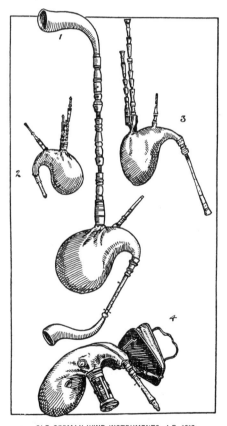

OLD GERMAN WIND INSTRUMENTS—A.D. 1619.

(1) *Large Bagpipe.* (2) *Dudey or Hornpipe.* (3) *Shepherd's Pipe.* (4) *Bagpipe with Bellows.*

So at this date there was a difference between the Highland pipes, the Lowland and the Hibernian. The instrument was, in fact, becoming recognised as peculiar to the Highlands, in the one specific form at least.

A.D. 1617 - When James I came to Scotland in 1617 and decorated Holyrood with images of many kinds, he did not clear out the bagpipes from the Palace, jokingly remarking that as they had some relation to the organ they might remain.

A.D. 1623 - Playing on the "great pipe" was a charge made against a piper at Perth in 1623. The term great pipe would seem to indicate that the instrument was evolved from a previous kind, and is an argument in favour of the theory that the pipes were not "introduced" into Scotland, but are of native origin, and have been gradually developed up to their present condition.

A.D. 1650 - "Almost every town hath bagpipes in it," says a writer of the year 1650.

A.D. 1700 - About the beginning of the eighteenth century the big drone was added to the bagpipe, distinguishing it henceforth from the Lowland and Northumbrian.

A.D. 1741 - On a political occasion in 1741 the Magistrates of Dingwall were welcomed home by the ringing of bells, "while young and old danced to the bagpipe, violin, and Jewish harp." Rather a curious medley they would make.

A.D. 1745 - Prince Charlie had a large number of pipers with him in his rebellion of 1745. After the battle of Prestonpans his army marched into Edinburgh, a hundred pipers playing the Jacobite air, "The King shall enjoy his ain again:" and when he marched to Carlisle he had with him a hundred pipers. Perhaps it was because of its prominence in his rebellion that the bagpipe was afterwards classed by the ruling powers as an instrument of warfare, the carrying of which deserved punishment.

A.D. 1755 - In this year we find the first reference to a professional maker of bagpipes. In the *Edinburgh Directory* for 1755, a book that could be carried in the vest pocket, "Hugh Robertson" is entered as "pipe maker, Castle Hill, Edinburgh."

It is not necessary to trace the instrument farther down through the years. In Scotland, after it overcame the set-back of the '45, it became more popular year by year until at last in 1824, we find an English traveller saying that "the Scots are enthusiastic in their love for their national instrument. In Edinburgh the sound of the bagpipe is to be heard in every street." The Lowland, the Northumberland and the Irish pipes lost favour, and the Lincolnshire - that referred to by Shakespeare - has been totally extinct since about 1850. The Great Highland Bagpipe is the only form that has held its own.

The early history of the Celts affords abundant room for controversy, and the origin of the pipes will always be debatable. The weight of evidence, however, goes to show that the pipes and pipe music are far more likely to have been evolved out of the life of the Highland people than imported from any other country.

The first thoroughly authentic reference to the bagpipe in Scotland dates from 1406, it was well known in Reformation times, the second drone was added about 1500, it was first mentioned in connection with the Gaelic in 1506, or a few years later, it was classed in a list of Scottish musical instruments in 1548, in 1549 and often afterwards it was used in war. In 1650 every town had a piper, in 1700 the big drone was added, and in 1824 the Scots were enthusiastic about the pipes. There is not the slightest doubt, of course, that the instrument was used in Scotland for many years, probably for centuries, before we can trace it, but previous to the dates given we have only tradition and conjecture to go by.

From 1700 to 1750 was perhaps the most critical time in the story of the Great Highland Bagpipe. The disaster at Culloden nearly spelt ruin for the pipes as well as for the tartan. The Disarming Act was very stringent, and the pipes came in for almost as strict a banning as did the kilt. The Jacobites were outlawed, the tartan was pronounced a mark of extreme disloyalty to the House of Hanover, and the life of a professed piper was hardly worth living. The Celt was crushed by the severity of his defeat and broken by the inrush of innovation that followed.

Clanship, as such, ceased, and the chiefs, from being the fathers of their people, become the landlords. The Highlander lost his reckless passions, but he also lost his rude chivalry and his absorbing love for the old customs.

But in 1782, the ban of the Disarming Act was removed, and the people were ready for new ideas. A spirit of improvement and an enthusiasm for things Highland appeared, first modestly, then boldly, and under the auspices of a renovated society, without the environments of war and romance, a new order asserted itself. Competitions stirred up the more clever of the piping fraternity, and further popularised the music, books on Highland piping, written or compiled by leading pipers, began to appear, and with the publication of histories of the many tunes, the people began to take an intelligent and patriotic interest.

THE OLDEST PIPE TUNES

Precise dates have been given for many tunes, but it is obvious enough that the writers giving them, though doubtless good pipers, were but little conversant with the facts of history. Very few, indeed, of the older tunes can be authenticated. With them it is truly a case of being lost in the mists of antiquity.

There was always a fine vein of music among the Celts, and they readily composed rhymes and tunes which powerfully affected the imagination and into their tunes they compressed the sentiments of past centuries, and the troubles and joys of everyday life. The birth of an heir to the ancient clan, the death of the chief, a victory in battle, the home-coming or departure of any notable personage, were all fit subjects for the genius of the clan piper. Where we can prove that the tune was composed when the incident, of which we know the date, occurred, we are on sure ground. When we cannot we are none the wiser. Each clan had its own music, almost all of high antiquity, and all of the class common to the Gael, but we can no more fix the origin of the music than we can fix the origin of the clan. The Munros have a pibroch composed on the battle of *Bealach na Broige*, an event which took place about 1350, and there is the tradition in the Clan Menzies that their piper played at Bannockburn, but in neither case is the matter of any use as history. "The Desperate Battle of Perth" is alleged to date from 1395, "The MacRaes' March" from 1477, and "MacIntosh's Lament" from 1526. In each case, however, tradition is the only original authority, and to tradition a hundred years are often as one day, and one day as a hundred years.

But the fact that we cannot fix exact dates does not impair the value of the stories, as stories. And it is as stories, traditions if you will, that we wish to recall them now, if only to show the atmosphere in which our pipe music lived and moved and had its being. The stories I believe are true, though I would not like to vouch for the accuracy of the names of characters and places in every instance, no more than for that of the dates. The incident recorded may have taken place at some other time, in some other place, and with some other people, and tradition may have mixed up names and figures.

"The MacRaes' March"

This is the oldest known pipe tune. The Lord of the Isles invaded Ross-shire about 1477 with a numerous army, and laid waste the country of the MacKenzies, burning a chapel at Contin. The MacKenzies took the field to protect their lands and property, and in an endeavour to recover the booty from the MacDonalds they asked the assistance of the MacRaes. The MacRaes joined them and the MacDonalds were defeated with great slaughter. In the ranks of the MacRaes there fought Duncan MacRae, an orphan, familiarly known by the name of *Suarachan*, a term of contempt. His prowess on this occasion was remarkable, and fully entitled him to higher consideration. He slew a notable man in the MacDonald ranks, and then calmly sat down on the body, as if no more was required of him. MacKenzie was astonished at the action of this ally of his, and exclaimed:-

"Why sit you so, when your help is so much needed?"

"If paid like a man, I will fight like a man," replied MacRae. "If everyone does as much as I have done the day is yours."

"Kill your two and you shall have the wages of two," said the chief.

Suarachan obeyed, and again sat down on the corpse.

"Kill your three," shouted the MacKenzie; "nay, fight on, and I will reckon with you for the dead."

Suarachan thereupon got up, and dealt fearful destruction among the MacDonalds, killing sixteen with his own hand, and thus proved his worth. He was ever afterwards held in high esteem, and became a leading man in the clan, acquiring the honourable name of "Duncan of the Axe." It was an axe he wielded with such dread purpose on the field of battle. The pibroch was composed in his honour and in memory of the conflict.

The resemblance between the story and that of Hal o' the Wynd in Scott's *Fair Maid of Perth* is too striking to pass unnoticed. Hal, at the battle on the North Inch of Perth, acted exactly as *Suarachan* did at Contin. Which is the original story, or whether the two are different stories it is hard to determine. It would be interesting to know where Sir Walter got the legend on which he based the Hal o' the Wynd incident.

"The MacIntosh's Lament"

On the authority of The MacIntosh himself, this tune dates from 1550. Writing in 1885 the chief said:- "The tune is as old as 1550 or thereabout. Angus MacKay in his pipe music book gives it 1526, and says it was composed on the death of Lauchlan, the fourteenth laird, but we believe that it was composed by the famous family bard MacIntyre, of the death of William, who was murdered by the Countess of Huntly in 1550. This bard had seen, within the space of forty years, four captains of the Clan Chattan meet with violent deaths, and his deep feeling found vent in the refrain:-

'MacIntosh the excellent
They have lifted.
They have laid thee
Low, they have laid thee.'

These are the only words in existence which I can hear of."

There is, however, another tradition connected with the tune. There was a prediction, believed among the clansmen, that the MacIntosh of that day would die through the instrumentality of his beautiful black steed, whose glossy skin shone as the raven's wing, and whose flowing mane and tail waved free as the wind itself. But the chief, whatever he felt, was determined to show his people that he treated the prediction lightly, and so he continued to ride his favourite, in spite of the entreaties of his friends. He rode him on the day of his marriage, and on the way to the church the horse became more than usually restive. He reared and plunged, and behaved so badly that the rider, losing control of himself and his horse, drew his pistol and shot the favourite dead. Another, a piebald horse, was procured, and the company proceeded to church. After the ceremony they returned by the way they had come, the bride and her maids on white ponies, and the bridegroom and his friends following. The chief's horse, in passing, shied at the body of the black horse, which lay by the wayside, and the rider was thrown to the ground and killed on the spot. A turn of the road hid the accident from those in front, and the bride, unconscious of what had happened, went on her way. She is said to have composed and chanted the air as, at the funeral, she moved at the head of the bier, marking the time by tapping on the coffin lid all the way to the grave, where she had to be torn away as the body was being lowered in.

"A Cholla Mo Run"

One of the earliest recorded instances of the bravery of a piper is contained in the annals of our own Highlands, and is inseparably connected with the tune known as *A Cholla Mo Run*. It may be as well to give the story here at full length. The hero was the piper of Coll Kitto, or left-handed Coll, who landed in Islay with the advance party of an expedition from Ireland, with instructions to take the Castle of Dunivaig by surprise, should he find that this could be attempted with any degree of success. The Campbells, however, had heard of the expedition, and they drew the party into an ambush and made them prisoners. All were hung off-hand, except the piper, who asked leave first to play a lament over his comrades. The chief of the Campbells had heard of the fame of this piper, and, being himself fond of music, he granted the request, taking care, however, to put cattle in the way of those of Coll Kitto's people who might follow the advance party, which would distract their attention, while his men could fall on them as they did on the others. The piper saw and understood the arrangements, and adapted his pibroch to the occasion, so that the warning and lamenting notes could not fail to be understood by his comrades. The chief of the Campbells also understood, and on finding himself over-reached he plunged his dirk into the piper, who smiled proudly even in death, for he knew he had saved his friends. The lamenting notes represented in this tune by "We are in their hands, we are in their hands," and the warning notes represented by "leave the cattle, leave the cattle," are exceedingly touching, and Coll Kitto, when he heard the pibroch, at once knew that his advance party was in trouble, and that the piper wished him to keep away from the island. Accordingly he turned his *birlins*, that is, boats, and left for a less dangerous locality.

"Duntroon's Salute"

Another tune - "Duntroon's Salute" - is mixed up with A *Cholla mo run* in a rather peculiar way, a way that suggests that the origin of the one is somehow being attributed to the other. Sir Alexander MacDonald, *Alister MacCholla Chiotaich*, so this story goes, made a raid on Argyll in 1644 (the dates are irreconcilable with the accepted facts of the two stories), and surrounded Duntroon Castle, with the object of cutting off every person inside in revenge for the murder of his father's piper. He himself, with a fleet of galleys, besieged the castle from the seaward side, and he ordered his piper to play the "MacDonald's March." Instead, however, the piper, on the spur of the moment, composed and played a war cry to alarm Duntroon. After saluting Duntroon and wishing him good health, he warned him of his danger, pointed out that the enemy were ready to attack him by sea and land, from right and left and front. The tune was understood on shore and also on board MacDonald's boat, and the poor piper was instantly hung from the yard-arm. MacDonald finding he could not reduce Duntroon, moved northward, following out his work of destruction. The tune composed and played on this occasion is still known as "Duntroon's Salute," and that there is some truth in the story is shown by the way in which it seems to represent the sound of waves breaking against rocks. The exact relations between its origin and that of *A Cholla mo run* would, however, do with a little clearing up. It may be mentioned as a fact that some years ago a body was found buried within Duntroon, which was evidently that of the piper referred to in the tradition. But how, then, did the piper come to be buried in Duntroon?

"The Campbells are Coming"

This tune dates so far back in the centuries that we fail to trace its origin. It has been the march of the clan for hundreds of years. There is an old Gaelic song sung to the air, which tradition says was the composition of a piper. This piper, in the course of his vocation, was at a wedding in Inveraray, where he was inhospitably treated. Smarting under a sense of injury, he composed the song:-

"I was at a wedding in the town of Inveraray,
I was at a wedding in the town of Inveraray,
I was at a wedding in the town of Inveraray,
Most wretched of weddings, with nothing but shell-fish,"
thus mercilessly lashing his churlish host.

The tradition, by the way, was so implicitly believed in, that the playing of the tune at a wedding, up to a comparatively recent date, was regarded as a premeditated insult.

SOME WORLD FAMOUS PIBROCHS

"MacCrimmon's Lament"

There are several reasons why this should be the best known of all pipe tunes, but the most important is the fact that it is, and must ever continue to be, inseparably associated with the famous pipers of Dunvegan. The tune was composed by a piper who was leaving home, and had a presentiment that he would never return, but it has often been used in other circumstances. In the evicting days, when Highlanders were compelled to emigrate from their native shores, the favourite air when they were embarking was "Cha Till Mi Tuille" (I'll return no more), and on many other mournful occasions the lament of the MacCrimmons was made the means of expressing the feelings of Highlanders. It was composed in 1746 by Donald *Ban* MacCrimmon, then piper to MacLeod of Dunvegan. Donald *Ban* was considered the best piper of his day, and when the clan left Dunvegan to join the Royalists in 1746, he was deeply impressed with the idea that he himself would never again see the old castle. The parting of the clansmen with their wives and children was sad, and Donald *Ban*, thinking of his own sweetheart, poured forth his soul in the sad wail of the Lament, as the MacLeods were marching away from the castle. The clan afterwards took part in a skirmish, which, from the peculiar circumstances, is known to history as the "Rout of Moy," and MacCrimmon was shot close by the side of his chief.

The Gaelic words usually associated with the lament are supposed to have been sung by Donald *Ban's* sweetheart, but they are in all likelihood of much later date. The chorus however, is probably as old as the tune, but the complete verses first appeared in print in 1835, in a collection of *Popular Gaelic Songs* by John MacKenzie, of the *Beauties of Gaelic Poetry*, where the words are said to have been taken from an old Skye manuscript.

If "MacCrimmon's Lament" is associated with a departure for the wars, there is another tune associated very closely with war itself - so closely, indeed that, according to the accepted story of its origin, it was composed while one of the most cruel deeds ever done in the name of warfare was being perpetrated.

"Gilliechroist" or "Killychrist"

This is the war tune of Glengarry, and its origin - mythical according to some writers - is as follows:-

About the beginning of the seventeenth century there lived in Glengarry a famous character named Allan MacRanald, of Lundie. He was a man of great strength, activity, and courage, and, living as he did at a time when the feuds between the MacKenzies and the MacDonalds were at their height, he invariably led any expedition that set out from Glengarry. In these fighting days young Angus MacDonald, of Glengarry, anxious to distinguish himself, determined - though against the advice of his father - to lead a raid into the country of the MacKenzies. He surprised and defeated the MacKenzies, but on their way home by sea the MacDonalds were in their turn attacked by the MacKenzies, and defeated with great slaughter. Angus MacDonald was among the slain, and Allan of Lundie only escaped with his life by leaping into the sea at Loch Hourn, where the battle took place, and swimming ashore at another place. Allan was determined to be avenged, and not long after he led a strong party of MacDonalds to the lands of Killychrist, near Beauly. He found the MacKenzies totally unprepared, burned their lands, destroyed their crops, and finally mercilessly set fire to a church in which a large congregation were worshipping, driving back at the point of the sword all who attempted to escape. Meantime he ordered Alister *Dubh*, his piper, to play so as to drown the cries of the perishing people. Alister thereupon blew up loud and shrill, and, after making his instrument give utterance to a long succession of wild and unconnected notes without any apparent meaning, he began his march round the church, playing extemporaneously the pibroch which, under the name of "Killychrist," has since been used as the war tune of the MacDonells of Glengarry. For a short time the terrible sounds from the inside of the church mingled with the music of the pipes, but they gradually became fainter, and at last ceased altogether.

Allan and his comrades had little time to enjoy their victory, for the MacKenzies soon gathered in overwhelming numbers, and, finding the MacDonells resting on a flat near Mealfourvonie, known as "the marsh of blood", they attacked them with great fury, and pursued them to Loch Ness. Allan was again one of the few who escaped.

The story of the burning in the church has been altogether discredited, but it is admitted that there was a raid, and that a large number of cottages, as well as the manse of Killychrist, were burnt. None of the earlier writers, however, mention the burning of the congregation. The music itself also contradicts somewhat the traditional origin of the tune, for when it is properly played the listener can fancy he hears the flames rustling and blazing through the timbers, mingled with the angry remonstrances and half-smothered shouts of the warriors, but there is no representation of the more feeble plaints of women and children, as there would surely have been had these been among the victims. However, I give the story for what it is worth.

"Piobaireachd Dhomhnuill Duibh"

This is one of the oldest and best known of pipe tunes. It is said to have been played at the Battle of Inverlochy in 1431, and it is first found on paper in Oswald's *Caledonian Pocket Companion*, published in 1764 where it is entitled *Piobaireachd Mhic Dhonuill*. Afterward it appeared in the book compiled by Captain MacLeod of Gesto, from which it was translated in 1815 into ordinary notation by the editor of *Albyn's Anthology*. Its first printed heading strengthens the title of the MacDonalds, who claim the tune for their clan, but the words *Donull Dubh* are accepted as referring to Cameron of Lochiel, and the tune is known as "Lochiel's March." The chief of the Camerons bears the name *MacDhomhnuill Duibh*, or son of Black Donald. The air, which is the march of the 79th or Cameron Highlanders, is a call to arms, and is inseparably associated with Inverlochy, but whether composed and played on the field or only in commemoration of the battle cannot now be determined.

"Is Fada Mar So Tha Sinn"

This may be translated "Too Long in this Condition," is an old pibroch, dating from about 1712. It was composed either by Donald *Mor* MacCrimmon or by Patrick his son. Donald was compelled at one time, because of some depredations of his own, to flee for his life into Sutherlandshire. There he put up unrecognised at the house of a relative named MacKay, who was getting married that day. MacCrimmon sat down in a corner almost unnoticed, but when the piper began to play he unconsciously fingered his stick as if it were the chanter. The piper of the evening noticed this, and asked him to play for them. Donald said he could not, and the whole company asked him, and he again refused. At last the piper said: "I am getting seven shillings and sixpence for playing at this marriage. I'll give you one-third if you will play." Donald then took up the pipe and began:-

"Too long are we thus, too long are we thus,
Too long in this condition,
Too long lacking meat or drink,
At MacKay's marriage am I."

These lines he repeated three times, and concluded by adding -

"At the house of MacKay am I."

He played so well that all present knew him to be the great Donald *Mor* MacCrimmon, and as he made his pipes speak to them they understood his complaint, and he was then royally entertained.

The pibroch is also said to have been composed by Patrick *Mor* MacCrimmon on his being taken prisoner, along with many others, at the battle of Worcester, and being left in a pitiable state. It is also associated with the same piper and the battle of Sheriffmuir, where he was left stripped of all his clothing, but it is impossible to say which, if either, is right.

ANGUS MAC KAY: FIRST PIPER TO QUEEN VICTORIA

"The Miserly, Miserable One's House"

Want of hospitality towards a piper gave rise to this tune, and its origin, as told to the late "Nether Lochaber" by an old Loch Awe-side piper, was as follows:-

Some two or three hundred years ago, when the great Clan Campbell was at the height of its power, the estate of Barbreck was owned by a

Campbell, who was brother or cousin or something of another Campbell, the neighbouring laird of Craignish. Craignish kept a piper, but Barbreck did not. Barbreck could afford to keep one, but he grudged the expense, and his stinginess in this respect is commemorated in an Argyllshire saying - "What I cannot afford I must do without, as Barbreck did without a piper."

Barbreck one day was on a visit to Craignish, and as he was leaving he met the piper, and said to him - "The New Year is approaching. On New-Year's Day morning, when you have played the proper salute to my cousin, your master, I wish you would come over to Barbreck and play a New-Year's salute to me, for, as you know, I have no piper of my own to do it. Come and spend the day with us." This the piper promised to do, and on New Year's Day morning, after first playing his master into good humour, he went to Barbreck. He played and played until the laird was in raptures, but the piper became hungry and thirsty, and hinted as much to Barbreck. He got some food, but it was not satisfactory, either in quantity or quality. The drinkables were no better, and long before the sun set the piper was anxious to go home. "Give us one more tune before you go," said Barbreck. "That I will," said the piper and there and then he struck up impromptu *Tigh Bhroinein* - the House of the Miserly One. The following are some of the lines attached to the tune from the very first, whether by the piper himself or by another is not known:-

"I was in the house of the miserly one today,
In the house of the miserly one was I;
I went by invitation thither,
But I got no sufficiency (or meat or drink).
I got a drink of meal gruel there,
And got bad barley scones;
I got the leg of a hen there,
And, by my troth, she was a poor and tough one.
This is an invitation that has annoyed me,
I will leave this to-night
Without (I may say) food or drink

I will leave thee, Barbreck;
Nor will I return any more
To play thee a piobaireachd salute."

The translation is too literal to be poetry, but one can imagine how Barbreck must have felt. He had better have done without that last tune.

"Oh, That I Had Three Hands!"

This is associated with at least two incidents in Highland history. Towards the end of the thirteenth century a dispute arose between *MacCailein Mor*, Chief of the Clan Campbell, and MacDougall of Lorne, chief of the MacDougalls, with reference to the boundaries of their estates. The parties met at a spot where two streams unite, and fell to recrimination and ultimately to fighting like tigers. The slaughter was terrible, and the streams ran with blood and were crowded with the bodies of the slain. Ultimately *MacCailein Mor* was killed, and his followers ceased the fighting to carry off his body. Close to the battlefield there was a small conical hillock - called in the Gaelic *Tom-a-Phiogbair*, the Piper's Hillock - on the top of which the piper of the Campbells stood and played while the battle raged. Sympathising with the MacDougalls, and regretting the havoc made among them, he composed on the spot a pipe tune. The Campbells, seeing that this was not one of their own tunes, were so enraged that one of them ran to the piper and chopped off his head.

The other incident connected by tradition with the tune is that later related of a cave either in Skye or Mull, into which a venturesome piper entered. He never returned, but the last wailing notes of his pipes told that he was being hard beset with wolves, who threatened to tear him to pieces should he stop playing. So he played mournfully:-

"Oh, that I had three hands!
Two for the pipes and one for the sword,"

the inference being that in that case he could have kept on playing and fought the wolves at the same time.

The tune nearly always played at Highland funerals is "Lochaber No More". It was composed to Jane, daughter of Sir Ewen Cameron of Lochiel, by a young English officer on his being ordered back from the Highlands to join his regiment. Jane Cameron was afterwards married to Lachlan MacPherson of Cluny, thus bringing over the tune to the MacPhersons. The traditional account is entirely different. According to it a party of marauders from Lochaber, consisting of forty to fifty men, reached, one autumn afternoon, the summit of a hill immediately above Glenesk. They meant to make a raid on the valley, but lay down to rest until after dusk. They were, however, seen by some shepherds, who gave the alarm, and in the evening the inhabitants of the glen were all under arms for the protection of their property. After dusk the invaders descended, and in the battle that ensued five of the defenders were killed and ten taken prisoner. Prisoners and cattle were driven to the Highlands. The men returned next year after a ransom of fifteen merks had been paid for each, but the cattle were never seen again.

"I Have Had a Kiss of the King's Hand."

Pipers of old times always had "a guid conceit o' themsel's," and Patrick *Mor* MacCrimmon, who flourished in 1660, was no exception to the rule. His master, Roderick MacLeod of MacLeod, went to London after the Restoration to pay his homage to Charles II, and was very warmly received. He had taken his piper with him, and the King was so pleased with his fine appearance and his music that he allowed MacCrimmon to kiss his hand. Patrick was highly elated over this, and commemorated the honour that had been paid by him composing the tune *Fhuair mi pog o laimh an Righ*, which, to those acquainted with the language and music, seems to speak forth the pride and gratitude of the performer, the words expressed by the opening measure being:-

"I have had a kiss, a kiss, a kiss,
I have had a kiss of the King's hand;
No one who blew in a sheep's skin
Has received such an honour as I have."

"Rory Mor's Lament."

Sir Roderick MacLeod of Dunvegan, who died somewhere about 1630, was a man of noble spirit, celebrated for great military prowess and resource. His hospitality was unbounded, and he was in all respects entitled to be called *Mor* or great, in all the qualities that went to constitute a great Highland chief and leader of men. The Gaelic bards were enthusiastic in his praises, and his piper, Patrick *Mor* MacCrimmon - the same MacCrimmon presumably - taking his death very much to heart, could not live at Dunvegan afterwards. Shouldering his great pipe, he made for his own house at Boreraig, composing and playing as he went *Cumha Ruaraich Mhoir* (Rory *Mor's* Lament), which is considered the most melodious, feeling, and melancholy lament known.

"The Clan Farlane Pibroch"

A story is told of Andrew, chief of the Clan MacFarlane, and the supposed composer of the "Clan Farlane Pibroch." Andrew and Alastair, chiefs of the MacDonells of Keppoch, were credited with having "the black art." They were said to have sold their souls to the devil in exchange for their supernatural powers. They seem to have driven a rather peculiar bargain, for the understanding was that the devil should get only one of their souls, the chiefs to decide between themselves which it would be. The appointed day and hour came on which the debt was to be paid, and still the chiefs, though they had come to the trysting place, had not decided which soul was to be given up. When the devil came he was in a desperate hurry, and at once exclaimed, "Well, and whose soul do I get?" On the spur of the moment MacDonell pointed to MacFarlane's shadow, saying, "That's he," whereupon the devil snatched up the shadow and ran off with it. From that day MacFarlane was never known to cast a shadow.

As to the tune itself, Sir Walter Scott supposes it had a close connection with the predatory excursions of the clan into the low country near the fastnesses on the western side of Loch Lomond.

"John Garbh of Raasay's Lament"

Connected with "John Garbh of Raasay's Lament," one of the most famous pibrochs, there are stories of pipers, poetry, and superstition. John Garbh MacLeod of Raasay met his death about 1650 at the early age of 21. He was a man of fine appearance and great strength. He had been to Lewis on a visit to a friend, and when he was returning home to Skye the day was so stormy that his crew were very unwilling to put to sea, being afraid they would lose their lives. Raasay thereupon exclaimed to the boatman in the Gaelic:- "Son of fair Muireil, are you afraid?" and the man at once threw his fears aside, and with the reply - "No, no, Raasay, we shall share the same fate to-day," began to prepare for the voyage. All went well until off Trotternish, the people of which anxiously watched the boat. The wind increased still more, and a heavy shower hid the vessel from their sight. When it cleared off the boat was nowhere to be seen. MacLeod's untimely fate was deeply mourned, and Patrick Mor MacCrimmon commemorated the sad event by composing the famous and pathetic pibroch.

THE PIPES IN BATTLE

The Duke of Cumberland, on seeing the pipes of clansmen who supported him at Culloden asked somewhat testily: "What are these men to do with such bundles of sticks. I can get far better implements of war that these." "Your Royal Highness," said an aide-de-camp, "cannot get them better weapons. They are the bagpipes, the Highlanders' music in peace and war. Without these all other instruments are of no avail, and the Highland soldiers need not advance another step, for they will be of no service." Then Cumberland who was too good a tactician to underrate the value of anything, allowed the pipers to take their part in the fight.

The use by the Celts of the bagpipes in battle fits in with all we know of the ancient people Their demeanour in the actual fight was always remarkable. In old times each warrior fought for his own hand, with his own claymore, subject to no system of rules. Before the battle a strange nervous excitement, called by ancient writers, *crithgaisge*, or "quiverings of valour," came over him. This was followed by an overpowering feeling of exhilaration and delight, called *mir-cath*, or "the joyous frenzy of battle." It was not a thirst for blood, but an absorbing idea that both his own life and fame and his country's good depended on his efforts, and a determination to do all that could be done by a resolute will and undaunted spirit. The *mir-cath* has been seen in a modified form on several occasions in modern warfare, but only when the Highland soldier has a chance of charging with the bayonet. Then that shout which precedes an onset no foe can withstand is heard, and the Highlanders forget themselves and rush forward like an irresistible torrent.

The first mention of military bagpipe music is given in accounts of the battle of Glenlivck, in 1594, but it is not until after 1600 that we find pipers mentioned as men of war by reputable historians. In 1627, says the Transactions of the Society of Antiquaries in Scotland, a certain Alex. MacNaughton of that ilk was commissioned by King Charles I to "levie and transport two hundredthe bowmen" to serve in the war against France. On January 15th 1628, he wrote to the Earl of Morton, from Falmouth, where his vessel had been driven by stress of weather. In a postscript he said:-

"My L.- As for newis from our selfis, our bagg pypperis and Marlit Plaidis serwitt us in guid wise in the pursuit of ane man of war that hetlie followit us."

In 1641, Lord Lothian, writing from the Scottish Army at Newcastle, puts in a word for the pipers:-

"I cannot out of our armie furnish you with a sober fiddler; there is a fellow here plays exceeding well, but he is intollerably given to drink; nor have we many of those people. Our armie has few or none that carie not armes. We are sadder and graver than ordinarie soldiers, only we are well provided of pypers. I have one for every company in my regiment, and I think they are as good as drummers."

They were evidently better than fiddlers, anyhow.

In 1642 there were regular regimental pipers, and it is believed that the 21st Royal Scots Fusiliers, then the North British Fusiliers, was about the first regiment which had them. When the town of Londonderry was invested in 1689 by James VII, two drums, a piper, and colours were allotted to each company of infantry, each troop of horse had a trumpet and a standard, and each troop of dragoons had two trumpets, two hautbois, and a standard. When the figures relating to the strength of the army are analysed, it is found that each regiment must have had fourteen pipers, fifty-six drums, five trumpets, and fourteen hautbois - that is, if the bands were at full strength.

That pipers were not always confined to the land forces is shown by an advertisement in the *Edinburgh Courant* in 1708, asking for "any person that plays on the bagpipes who might be willing to engage on board a British man-of-war." British and Dutch ships are known to have been lying in Leith Roads at the time, which accounts for the advertisement. A harper is mentioned as being in the navy as early as 1660, so music was not a new thing on board a man-of-war.

Although drummers were used in Highland regiments before 1745, the pipers outnumbered them very much, for whenever one was found who could play the pipes, the clans compelled him to follow them. Prince Charlie is said to have had thirty-two, who played before his tent at mealtime, and that their instrument was considered a weapon of war is proved by the fact that although a James Reid, one of the pipers who was taken on the suppression of the rebellion, pleased that he had not carried arms, and was not, therefore, a soldier, the Courts decided that the pipe was a warlike instrument, and punished the performer just as if he had carried a claymore. When, after the battle of Prestonpans, the Prince entered Edinburgh, we read that -

"As he came marching up the street,
The pipes played loud and clear,
And a' the folks came running out
To meet the Chevalier."

At the time of the rebellion the pipers had come to be highly respected members of the clans. Almost as much so as the bards were in their day. In 1745 the MacLeods marched into Aberdeenshire and were defeated at Inverurie. MacCrimmon, the great piper from Dunvegan, and master of the celebrated Skye "college," was taken prisoner after a stout resistance, and the following morning it was found that not one of the pipers of the victorious army played through the town as usual. When asked the reason they answered that while the MacCrimmon was in captivity their instruments would not sound, and it was only on the release of the prisoner that they resumed their duties. The MacCrimmons were then, however, so well known all over the Highlands that the action of the other pipers can hardly be considered remarkable.

Many and many a time has the efficacy of pipe music in rallying men and leading them on to victory been proved. At Quebec in April, 1760, when Fraser's regiment were retreating in great disorder the general complained to a field officer of the behaviour of his corps. "Sir," the officer replied, warmly, "you did very wrong in forbidding the pipers to play this morning; nothing encourages the Highlanders so much in the day of battle, and even now they would be of some use." "Then," said the general, "let them blow like the devil if that will bring back the men." The pipers played a favourite martial air, and the Highlanders, the moment they heard it, re-formed and there was no more disorder.

When the regiment raised by Lord MacLeod in 1778, called the 73rd or MacLeod's Highlanders, was in India, General Sir Eyre Coote thought at first that the bagpipe was a "useless relic of the barbarous ages and not in any manner calculated to discipline troops." But the distinctness with which the shrill sounds made themselves heard through the noise of battle and the influence they seemed to exercise induced him to change his opinion. At Port Novo in 1781, he, with eight thousand men, of which the 73rd was the only British regiment, defeated Hyder Ali's army of twenty-five battalions of infantry, four hundred Europeans, from forty-thousand to fifty thousand horse, and over one hundred thousand matchlock men, with forty-seven canon. The 73rd was on the right of the first line, leading all the attacks, and the general's notice was particularly attracted by the pipers, who always blew up the most war-like strains when the fire was hottest. This so pleased Sir Eyre Coote that he called out - "Well done, my brave fellows, you shall have a set of silver pipes for this." And he was as good as his word, for he gave the men £50, and the pipes which this bought had an inscription testifying to the high opinion the general had of the pipers.

At the battle of Assaye, again, the musicians were ordered to lay aside their instruments and attend to the wounded. One of the pipers who obeyed this order was afterwards reproached by his comrades. Flutes or hautbois, they told him, they could well spare, but for the piper, who should always be in the heat of the battle, to go to the rear, with the whistles was a thing unheard of. The unfortunate piper was quite humbled, but he soon had an opportunity of playing off the stigma, for in the advance at Argaun shortly after, he played with such animation that the men could hardly be restrained from breaking the line and rushing to the charge before the time.

On a different nature is a story told of the Seaforth Highlanders. On the 12th August, 1793, as the grenadiers of Captain Gordon's company at Pondicherry were on duty in the trenches, exposed to a burning sun and cannon-fire from a fortress nearby, Colonel Campbell, field officer of the trenches, ordered the piper to play some pibrochs. This was considered a strange order but it was immediately complied with, and, says the writer of the chronicles of the regiment, "we were a good deal surprised to perceive that the moment the piper began, the fire from the enemy slackened, and soon almost entirely ceased. The French all got upon the works, and seemed more astonished at hearing the bagpipes than we with Colonel Campbell's request." It was a new kind of warfare, and again justifies the use of the appellation "weapon" instead of "instrument" used by the court which tried the Jacobite piper in 1746.

Bonnie Prince Charlie began to fear that all was lost when the clans failed to rally to his standard at Glenfinnan. But on the afternoon of August 19 the sound of the pipes made themselves heard, and shortly after the clans appeared. This is the moment which the authoress of the well-known song, "The March of the Cameron Men," has described:-

"Oh proudly they walk, but each Cameron knows
He may tread on the heather no more,
But boldly he follows his chief to the field,
Where his laurels were gathered before.
"I hear the pibroch sounding, sounding,
Deep o'er the mountain and glen,
While light springing footsteps are trampling the heath,
'Tis the march of the Cameron men."

PIPERS AND FAIRIES

Their association with fairies provides the most interesting of all the stories about pipers. There are ever so many stories of their adventures in the fairies' mounds and caves, and, like other classes of Celtic tales, they all run in one groove though they are located as far distant as Scotland is long. Like the story of *Faust*, where a man sells his soul for a period of worldly pleasure, so the story of the piper who goes to the fairies for a while, and sometimes comes back again, permeates all the literature of its class. It turns up all over Scotland.

Perhaps the most concise version of the fairy story comes from Sutherland. A man whose wife had just been delivered of her first-born set off with a friend to the village of Lairg to have the child's birth entered in the session books, and to buy a cask of whisky for the christening. As they returned, weary with the day's walk, they sat down to rest at the foot of the hill of Durcha, on the estate of Rosehall, near a large hole, from which they were ere long astonished to hear the sounds of piping and dancing. The father, feeling very curious, entered the cavern, went in a few steps, and disappeared. The other man waited for a while, but had to go home without his friend. After a week or two had passed, and the christening was over, and still there was no sign of the father's return, the friend was accused of murder. He denied the charge again and again, and repeated the tale of how the child's father had disappeared into the cavern. At last he asked for a year and a day in which to clear himself of the charge. He repaired often at dusk to the fatal spot and called for his friend, and prayed, but the time allowed him was all spent except one day, and nothing had happened. In the gloaming of that day, as he sat by the hillside, he saw what seemed to be his friend's shadow pass into the opening. He followed it, and, passing inside, heard tunes on the pipes, and saw the missing man tripping merrily with the fairies. He caught him by the sleeve and pulled him out. "Bless me, Sandy!"" cried the father, "why could you not let me finish my reel." "Bless me!" replied Sandy, "have you not had enough of reeling this last twelvemonth?" "Last twelvemonth!" cried the other in amazement, nor would he believe the truth concerning himself till he found his wife sitting by the door with a year-old child in her arms. The time passed quickly in the company of the good people.

Here again, is perhaps the best of the long stories of pipers and fairies. It is from the *Celtic Magazine*, so ably conducted by the late Alexander MacKenzie:-

"Jamie Gow", a celebrated piper of many, many years ago, lived at Niskisher, in Harris. He had a croft, but neglected it for the pipes, which brought him his livelihood. His home was five miles from a famous fairy knoll, in which thousands of fairies were. Till Jamie's time no one ever found the entrance. It was said that if a piper played a certain tune three times round the base of the knoll, going against the sun, he would discover the door, but this no hero of the chanter had previously attempted.

"Among a number of drouthy neighbours one day a debate got up as to the nature of the inside of the knoll. Jamie Gow declared that he would for a gallon of brandy play round the knoll in the proper way, and if he found the door he would enter and play the fairies a tune better than anything they had ever danced to. A score of voices cried "done," and the bargain was made. About noon on the following day, Jamie, after partaking of something to keep his courage up, proceeded to *Tom-na-Sithichean*, the Fairy Knoll. He was accompanied by scores of people, some cheering, some discouraging him. On reaching the knoll he emptied other two "coggies", took up his position, and began to play. As soon as the first skirl of his pipes was heard all the people fled to the top of an adjoining hill to wait the result. With a slow but steady step Jamie marched round the *Tom*. Twice he completed his journey without mishap, and he had almost finished the third round. But when within two or three paces of the end he was seen to stand for a moment and then disappear. There was an opening in the side of this hill, which admitted him to a long dark passage, so rugged and uneven as to make it most inconvenient for a piper to keep marching and playing a particular tune, as Jamie was. The air, too was chilly and disagreeable, drops of water continually trickling down the cold damp sides of the passage. Jamie, however, marched on fearlessly, and strange to say the farther he went the lighter grew his step and the livelier his tune. By and by the long passage became illuminated with a faint light, by which he saw that the roof and sides were very thickly covered with short and starry pendants, which shone white and radiant, like marble. Forward still, till he reached a door which opened of its own accord and led into a chamber of indescribable splendour. The floor seemed of solid silver, the walls of pure gold, and the furniture most costly. Around the table sat hundreds of lovely women and smiling men, all perfect in form and clothed in spotless green, brilliant and rich beyond description. They had apparently finished a sumptuous dinner, and were now quaffing the purple juice of the grape out of diamond-mounted cups of exquisite beauty.

A MAC ARTHUR PIPER

"At the sight of such splendour, the piper for a moment was amazed, the drones fell powerless on his arm, for he stood with open mouth, ceasing to blow his bag. Noticing this, one of the green gentlemen rose from his seat, and, smiling coyly, handed him a cup of wine to drink, which Jamie loved too dearly to refuse. So, taking the proffered cup, with thanks, he said -"I am a piper to my trade. I have travelled and played from one end of the island to the other, but such a pretty place and such lovely people I never saw." And he quaffed the cup at one draught.

"The gentleman in green then asked if he would favour the company with a tune called 'The Fairy Dance,' at which they knew he excelled all other performers. Nothing pleased Jamie better than a little puffing, - this probably, the inhabitants of the knoll knew - and he replied lustily. 'And, by my faith, I will, and I will play it as true as ever any piper played a tune.' In a moment the vast assembly was on its feet, swinging from side to side in a long country dance. Nothing that Jamie had ever seen compared to the graceful manner in which both ladies and gentlemen performed their evolutions, and this encouraged him to blow with might and main and stamp hastily with both feet, as if inspired, like the other performers.

"Meanwhile the people who had accompanied Jamie surrounded the knoll in search of him. They saw the spot where he disappeared, and some asserted that they saw the door itself, but when they came near the place there was no door. They continued the search for weeks, looking and listening in the hope of hearing the well-known notes of his chanter, but without success. Years passed, and Jamie did not return. The story of his disappearance at the knoll had spread far and wide, and his fate was the subject of conversation at many gatherings throughout the Western Isles. But though he was sadly missed at the balls and weddings, no one missed or pined for Jamie like his widowed mother and his sweetheart, *Mairi Nighean Gilleam*, to whom he was to have been married shortly after he left on his rash journey round the knoll.

"For several years Jamie continued to play 'The Fairy Dance,' and the dancers seemed as fresh as when he began. At long last the piper, wearied almost out of breath, cried 'May God bless you, friends! my breath is almost gone.' The mention of the Great Name produced a revolution. In a moment all lights were out, the beautifully clad assemblage and the gorgeous hall immediately disappeared, and Jamie found himself standing on the top of Tomnahurich at Inverness. Until he inquired at a cottage in the vicinity he was entirely ignorant of his surroundings, but as soon as he found out where he was he made direct for Harris, reaching there after a journey of six weeks.

"Jamie was seven years with the fairies. When he got back to Harris he found his cottage deserted, for his mother had died a year before. No one in the place recognised him, he was so changed. His beard reached to his girdle, his cheeks were bulged out to a prodigious size by continual blowing of his pipes, and his mouth was twice its original proportions. *Mairi Nighean Gilleam* knew him by his voice, and a few weeks after they became man and wife. Jamie never again visited Tom-na-Sithichean."

I should think not. He had had quite enough of the fairies. They, however, seem to have had a soft side to pipers, at least we often read of them helping the musicians with their music. The first story which illustrates this comes from one of the Inner Hebrides, and is given in J. F. Campbell's *Tales of the West Highlands*, the actual words of the narrator being used. It was told in a houseful of people, all of whom seemed to believe it:-

"There was a piper in this island and he had three sons. The two eldest learned the pipes, and they were coming on famously, but the youngest could not learn at all. At last, one day, he was going about in the evening very sorrowfully, when he saw *bruth*, a fairy hillock, laid open. (There was one close to the house, which was exactly like the rest of its class. It was afterwards levelled and human bones were found in it.) He went up to the door and stuck his knife into it, because he had heard from old people that if he did that the *slaugh* could not shut the door. Well, the fairies were very angry, and asked him what he wanted, but he was not a bit afraid. He told them he could not play the pipes a bit, and asked them to help him. They gave him *feadan dubh*, a black chanter, but he said: 'That's no use to me for I don't know how to play it.'

"Then they came about him and showed him how to move his fingers; that he was to lift that one and lay down that, and when he had been with them a while he thanked them and took out his knife and went away, and the *bruth* closed after him.

"Now, that man become one of the most famous pipers, and his people were alive until very lately. I am sure you all know that."

Chorus - "Oh yes, yes indeed. It is certain that there were such people whether they are now or not."

If all tales be true, the fairies had something to do with the eminent genius of the MacCrimmons themselves. Once upon a time, to use the proper phrase, there was a great gathering of the clans at Dunvegan Castle. MacLeod was entertaining the chiefs, and each chief was accompanied by his piper. The chiefs were great and the pipers were great, and somehow it was agreed that there should be a trial of skill among the musicians present - twelve in all. MacLeod himself directed the proceedings, and one by one the great instrumentalists stepped into the hall and made the rafters dirl with their well known strains. But MacLeod became anxious as he noticed that there was no sign of his own piper, the old piper who had served him so long. He sent a boy to search, and the boy returned with the sad news - the piper was hopelessly drunk. The brow of MacLeod grew dark with anger, for he was not to be humbled in his own household and in the presence of his guests. The tenth piper was tuning up - there was but another, and then his disgrace would be public property. In the desperation of despair MacLeod seized the boy by the hand and whispered: "You are the twelfth piper, remember your chief's words." The boy, MacCrimmon by name left the hall, while the feasting and fun went on as merrily as ever, and lay down on the hillside and bemoaned his fate. But his good fairy was not far away. She came right out of the ground, as pretty a little fairy as ever helped poor mortal in desperate plight. She knew his trouble, and did not waste words, but gave the distracted boy a curiously-shaped whistle, and bade him play on it. The youngster would do anything to oblige the kind lady, so he blew on the whistle, and lo! the hills and the rocks re-echoed with the finest music ever heard in Skye. The good fairy disappeared, and the boy ran back to the castle, where the eleventh piper was playing the last notes of his pibroch. The chiefs and pipers laughed to see the boy step it out into the centre of the assembled company, but their scorn was turned to admiration as compositions played in faultless and brilliant manner poured from the boy's "pipes." Thenceforth MacCrimmon was prince of pipers and we do not read that ever the good fairy came back to claim recompense for what she had done: neither have we any explanation of why she gave him a whistle and not a set of

SUPPOSED TO REPRESENT A MAC CRIMMON PLAYING A SALUTE
(From *Mac Ian's Clans.*)

pipes right off.

Another story of the MacCrimmons, but one that has not many points of resemblance to the other, is told by Lord Archibald Campbell in *Records of Argyll*. It is from the lips of Hector MacLean, of Islay, and tells of how, when MacDonald of the Isles resided in the palace on Finlagan Isle, in Loch Finlagan, he had a ploughman who, from his large stature, was called the Big Ploughman. This ploughman was out one day at his work, and he had a boy with him driving the horses, as was the custom in those times. The Big Ploughman was seized with hunger, and he said to the boy:

"My good fellow, were it to be got in the ordinary way, or magically, I would take food in the meantime, were I to have it."

After he had said these words, he and the boy took another turn with the team, till they came to the side of Knockshainta. There was an old grey-haired man by the side of the hill, who had a table covered with all manner of eatables. He asked them to come and partake of what was on the table. The ploughman went, but the boy was frightened, and would not go. After the ploughman had eaten enough, the old man gave him a chanter to play. When he put his fingers to it, he, who had never played before, played as well as any piper that ever was in the island of Islay. A day or two after, MacDonald, heard, in his palace on Island Finlagan, the Big Ploughman playing the Black Chanter. He inquired who it was, and they told him it was the Big Ploughman. When he heard how well the ploughman played there was nothing for it but to get for him the bagpipe of the three drones, and he was MacDonald's piper as long as he lived.

MacDonald went on a trip to the Isle of Skye. He took with him from thence a young man of the name of MacCrimmon, who was fond of music, and was doing a little at it. He went to the Big Ploughman to learn more music from him than he had already. MacCrimmon and the ploughman's daughter began courting and in consequence of the fancy that the girl took to MacCrimmon - believing that he would marry her - she took the Black Chanter unknown to her father out of the chest, and gave it to MacCrimmon to try it. When MacCrimmon tried it he could play as well as the Big Ploughman himself. The girl asked the chanter back, but he entreated her to let him have it for a few days until he should practise a little further on it. A short time after MacDonald of the Isles went off to Skye, and MacCrimmon went with him. He did not return the chanter, neither did he come back to marry the Big Ploughman's daughter. The people of Islay say it was in this way that the music went from Islay to the Isle of Skye.

"The Powers" were not always so unselfishly inclined as the stories already given make them appear. They often drove a Faust-like bargain with the piper. They did with Peter Waters, a Caithness lad, who, when driving home his cattle one day over the common in the parish of Olrig, stopped to quench his thirst at a spring which flowed from the side of a well-known fairies' hillock called Sysa. Peter was tired, the spot was quiet, and the air invited him to slumber. So he slept till near sunset, when he was awakened by a gentle shake of the shoulder. Starting up, he saw a most beautiful lady, dressed in green, with golden ringlets, blue eyes, and the sweetest countenance in the world, standing beside him. Peter was shy, and his first impulse was to run away, but the lady looked at him and he couldn't.

"Don't be afraid of me, Peter," she said, with one of her most captivating smiles, and with a voice soft and clear as a silver bell. "I feel a great interest in you, and I am come to make a man of you."

"I am much obliged to you, indeed," stammered Peter. "The greatest nobleman in the land might be proud of your fair hand, but I have no desire to enter into the silken cord; and, besides, I would require to be better acquainted with you before I took such a step. People commonly court a little before they marry."

The lady laughed.

"You mistake me altogether," said she. "Though you appear a very nice young man, I make no offer of my hand. What I mean is that I will put you in the way of rising in the world and making your fortune. Here are two things - a Book and a pipe. Make your choice of the one or the other. If you take the Book you will become the most popular preacher in the north, and if you take the pipe you will be the best piper in Scotland. I shall give you five minutes to consider," and she took from her bosom a golden time-piece about the size of a sovereign.

The book was a splendidly bound Bible, richly embossed with gold, and with a golden clasp; the pipe a beautiful instrument with a green silk bag of gold and silver tissue, and superbly finished with a number of silver keys. Peter gazed in admiration on the articles, and was greatly puzzled. It would be a grand thing, he thought, to be a popular preacher, to have a manse and glebe, and be fit company for the laird and his lady. But he was an enthusiast for music, and he should like above all things to be able to play the bagpipe. So he said -

"Since you are so kind, I think I will choose the pipe; but as I have never fingered a chanter in my life, I fear it will be a long time before I learn to play such a difficult instrument."

"No fear of that," said the lady. "Blow up, and you'll find that the pipe of its own accord will discourse the most eloquent music."

Peter did as he was desired, and lo! he played "Maggie Lauder" in splendid style - so splendidly that the cattle nearby began capering about in the most extraordinary manner.

"This is perfectly wonderful," he said. "There must surely be some glamour about this instrument."

He thanked the lady, and was about to take his departure, when she stopped him saying:

"There is a condition attached to the gift. This day seven years, at the very same hour in the evening, you must meet me by moonlight at the Well of Sysa. Swear by its enchanted spring that you will do so."

Peter was elated over his new acquisition, and rashly swore as she desired. Then he went home to his father's farm, the "Windy Ha'." With an air of triumph he produced his pipes, which excited much curiosity, and were greatly admired. But when he told how he came by them, the old people were fearful.

"It's no canny, Peter," said his father, shaking his head, "and I would advise you to have nothing to do with it."

"The Best protect us!" exclaimed his mother, "my bairn is lost. He must have got it from none other than the Queen of the Fairies."

"Nonsense," said Peter; "it was not the Queen of the Fairies, but a real lady - and a kind and beautiful lady she was - that gave me the pipes."

"But of what use can they be to you," said his father, "when you canna play them?"

"I'll let you see that," Peter replied, and, putting the wind pipe to his mouth, he played the "Fairy Dance" in a style that electrified the household. The whole family, including the grandmother, ninety years of age, started to their feet, and danced heartily, overturning stools and scattering the fire, which was in the middle of the floor, with their fantastic movements. The piper played as if he would never stop.

At length his father, panting for breath and with the perspiration running down his cheeks, cried out, "For mercy's sake, Peter, gie ower, or you'll be the death o' me and yer mither, as well as poor old grannie."

"I think," said Peter, laying aside his pipes, "I think you'll no longer say that I cannot play," and from that time his fame as a piper spread rapidly, and he was sent for to perform at weddings and merrymakings all over the country, till he realised a small fortune. But the seven years soon rolled away, and the afternoon arrived when he must keep his appointment with the donor of the pipes. Rover, the house dog, attempted to follow him, and when he was sent back he gazed after his master as far as he could see him, and then howled long and piteously. The evening was just such another as that seven years before, and the hillock of Sysa seemed, in the yellow radiance of the setting sun, to glow with unearthly splendour. Peter went, but he never returned, and the general belief was that he was carried away to Fairyland. At any rate, he was never again seen at Windy Ha'.

DEMON PIPES AND PIPERS

It was not at all a new idea that of Burns, when he represented the arch-enemy of mankind playing the pipes to the revellers in Alloway's "auld haunted kirk." The ancients had it, and the sylvan divinity Pan, who can be identified with the Satan of Scottish superstition, is said to have appeared as a performer on the bagpipe. A flute with seven reeds was his favourite instrument, and this may be identified with the bagpipe of tradition. Popular belief in the seventeenth century labelled the pipes as the Devil's favourite musical instrument. In 1679 some unhappy women were burned at Bo'ness for sorcery, and they were accused, among other things, "of meeting Satan and other witches at the cross of Murestane, above Kinneil, where they all danced, and the Devil acted as piper." Satan is also alleged to have acted in the same capacity in the guise of a rough, tawny dog at a dance on the Pentland Hills. MacMhurich, the bard of Clan Ranald, composed a Gaelic satire on national music, in which the "coronach of women" and *piob gleadhair*, the pipe of clamour, are called "the two ear sweethearts of the black fiend - a noise fit to rouse the imps," and there is a story connected with Glasgow Cathedral which shows further the prevalence of the idea. The gravestones round the Cathedral lie so close that one cannot walk across the ground without treading on them. This however, has not always been able to prevent resurrections, as would appear from the legend. Somewhere about the year 1700 a citizen one morning threw the whole town into a state of inexpressible horror and consternation by giving out that in passing at midnight through the kirkyard he saw a neighbour of his own, lately buried, rise out of his grave and dance a jig with the devil, who played the air of "Whistle ower the lave o't" on the bagpipe. The civic dignitaries and ministers were so scandalised at the intelligence that they sent the town drummer through the streets next morning forbidding any to whistle, sing or play the infernal tune in question.

A story curiously like that of Tam o'Shanter, but of a much more pleasant nature, at least for the human participator, comes from the Hebrides - the particular isle is not stated. A gentleman innkeeper, who was taught by Angus MacKay, the late Queen's piper, and could play the pipes as well as the violin, was sadly addicted to drink, and had frequent fits of *delirium tremens*, in which he had extraordinary experiences. Once when he had been indulging with his usual prodigality, the result found him in a large hall, laid out for dancing, and with a band of performers dressed in blue. The chief of the blue imps stood as if in front of the orchestra, grinning, capering, and gesticulating in the most fantastic manner. In the course of time, however, he became more amiable, and, drawing up his tail over his shoulder, he fingered it as if it were the chanter of the pipes, and there poured out a most inspiriting jig, the force of which neither demon nor man could resist, and the performance rivalled that in Alloway's "auld haunted kirk." But, and this is where Tan o' Shanter failed and the innkeeper succeeded, "mine host" remembered the tune after his recovery, and played it, and the last teller of the story says he "heard it played by another party who had learned it from him." But, unfortunately, he was too lazy to make a copy, so the "Lost Jig" went the way of the "Lost Pibroch," and is now unknown to the world.

That the idea of a demoniac piper is not peculiar to Scotland is shown by the sculpture executed by the celebrated German artist, Durer, which represents the Devil playing on the pipes; by an engraving of a pageant at Antwerp in the sixteenth century, where a similar figure occurs, and by various Continental stories and pictures. The pipes were, it should be added, far more often associated with religious matters than with demoniacal. The figure on the "apprentice pillar" in Rosslyn Chapel is that of a cherub playing on a Highland bagpipe, and, as has been shown in a previous article, there are many indications in ecclesiastical architecture and in ecclesiastical history that the pipes were not altogether banned from associating with the good. After the Reformation, it is true, they were held to be the Devil's instruments, and between 1570 and

1624 pipers were severely persecuted; but the zeal of the reformers, while always praiseworthy, often outran their discretion, and in their condemnation of instrumental music they included all minstrels. They vested supernatural powers in things which we now look upon as ordinary. The miseries of the Civil War were foretold by the appearance of a monster in the River Don, the disappearance of gulls from the lakes near Aberdeen, the loud tucking of drums in Mar, and in a seaman's house at Peterhead, where trumpets and bagpipes and tolling of bells gave additional horror to the sound.

The Clan Chisholm preserves, or at least did at one time preserve a relic believed to be of great antiquity. It is a chanter which is supposed to have a peculiar faculty of indicating the death of the chief by spontaneously bursting, and after each fracture it is carefully repaired by a silver fillet, which is an improvement on the original method of mending with a leathern thong. The family piper, when from home at a wedding, heard his chanter crack, and at once started up, saying he must return, for The Chisholm was dead. And he was.

But the most famous of all such articles is "The Black Chanter of Clan Chattan." This is a relic of the fight between the Clan Quhele and the Clan Yha on the North Inch of Perth in 1396. It is made of *lignum vitae*, and, according to tradition is endued with magical powers. About the end of the battle, so the tradition goes, an aerial minstrel was seen hovering over the heads of the Clan Chattan, who, after playing few wild notes on his pipes, let them drop to the ground. Being made of glass, they all broke except the chanter, which was made of wood. The Clan Chattan piper secured the chanter, and, though mortally wounded, he continued playing the pibroch of his clan until death silenced him. Some traditions say the original chanter was made of crystal, and, being broken by the fall, that now existing was made in exact facsimile, others that the cracks now seen were those the chanter received on falling to the ground. In any case, the possession of this particular chanter was ever after looked on as ensuring success, not only to the MacPhersons, but to any one to whom it happened to be lent. The Grants of Strathspey once received an insult, through the cowardice of some unworthy members of their clan, and in their dejection they borrowed the Black Chanter, the war notes of which roused their drooping energies and stimulated them to such vigour that it became a proverb from that time, "No one ever saw the back of a Grant." The Grants of Glenmoriston afterwards received it, and they restored it to the MacPhersons about 1855.

The Black Chanter seems to have kept its magic power, for, during all the troubles of the '45, Cluny MacPherson accompanied Prince Charlie in his victories and helped him much by his own and his followers' bravery. But when the final blow was given to the fortunes of Charles Edward at Drummossie Moor, the MacPhersons were not there, and it is said that before the battle an old witch told the Duke of Cumberland that if he waited until the green banner and the Black Chanter came up he would be defeated. The battle was over before Cluny arrived, for he was met by the fugitives when on his way from Badenoch to join the Prince. The MacIntoshes, who claim that their chief is the chief of the Clan MacPherson, were at Culloden and in the thickest of the fight, but they had not the Black Chanter, and so they, too, shared in the defeat. It is certainly curious that no battle at which the MacPhersons were present with the green banner of the clan, the Black Chanter, and the chief at their head, was lost.

PIPERS IN ENCHANTED CAVES

The story of a piper endeavouring to explore a mysterious cave is so closely allied to the class dealt with in the last chapter, that all might quite fairly have been included under one heading. The only difference often is that in the one case the piper enters a cave opening out to the sea, whereas is the other he enters a knoll, which may be any distance inland. There are always fairies in the knoll, but in the majority of cases there are none in the cave. Their place is taken by wild beasts, who take the life of the venturesome explorer. The piper generally has a dog with him when he enters the cave, and the dog always returns, though the last that is heard of his master is the sad wail of his pipes playing a lament for his own terrible fate.

"Oh, that I had three hands - two for the pipes and one for the sword," is recorded as the tune played by a piper who entered a cavern and could not get out again. The incident is located in several places - in Skye, in Mull, and at a cave eight miles up the River Nevis, in Inverness-shire. The Mull cave reached, it was believed, right across the island, and it was inhabited by wolves and other wild animals. The Skye cave was called *Uamh an Oir*, the Cave of Gold and was situated about four miles from Dunvegan, the other end opening out at Monkstad on Loch Snizort. It, too, had wild animals for inhabitants. The inside of the cave in most cases consisted of many confusing offshoots leading in different directions, the want of knowledge of which prevented the people of the neighbouring districts from exploring it. However, on one occasion a piper (the Skye version makes him a MacCrimmon) accompanied by a member of the Clan MacLeod (also the Skye version) made bold to enter the cave. A crowd gathered outside to wait for the result. The piper, who of course had his pipes, went first, playing his best. After a considerable time had elapsed, the waiting people began to feel anxious as to their safety. But by and by MacLeod returned. He could give no account of MacCrimmon except that he had lost him in the labyrinths of the cave.

He considered himself extremely fortunate in finding his way out. Their torches had been extinguished by the dim and foul atmosphere. Just when MacLeod was telling his story the wailing notes of MacCrimmon's pipes were heard issuing from the cave. All listened, and as they listened the pipes spoke, and the notes that came out of the darkness represented:-

"I will return, I will return, I will return no more;
MacLeod may return, but MacCrimmon shall never."

And also:-

"The she wolf, the she wolf, the she wolf follows me;
Oh for three hands; two for the pipes and one for the sword."

And so on the wailing notes continued, the piper bewailing his fate in that he could not stop his playing for an instant, because if he did this the wolf would attack him. So long as he played he was safe. Ultimately he began to speak of how long his strength would last, sometimes coming near to the mouth of the cave, but anon wandering away again into its recesses till the music was scarcely audible. This went on all that day and night but in the early morning the listeners heard the music cease, and they knew that exhaustion had overtaken the piper, and that the wolf had conquered.

The Mull story is told of two of a wedding party who entered the cave and never came out, and also of twelve men of the Clan MacKinnon, who, headed by a piper, attempted to explore the cave. In the latter case another party walked along the top keeping pace with the music below. When the party who travelled in the cave arrived at the end, the fact was to be signalled to those outside by a certain bar of music, and they were to mark the spot to indicate the termination of the cave. After the explorers had travelled some distance they encountered a fairy woman, who attacked the band and slew them one by one. She was, however, so charmed with the music of the pipes that she offered no injury to the person who played them. The poor piper made the best of his way back to the mouth of the cave followed by the fairy, she meanwhile informing him that if he ceased playing before he saw the light of day he too would be killed. He staggered along in the dark, bravely playing out his life breath, but at last, in spite of his struggles, the music ceased. The charm was then broken and the piper shared the fate of his comrades. Those outside knew that something had happened and with drawn swords rushed into the cave. They found the dead piper and his comrades. The last notes he played, says the tradition, were-

"Alas! that I had not three hands -
Two for the pipes and one for the sword."

This identifies the story as just a variation of the others, though how it comes to be located in so many different places it is difficult to explain. In connection with the MacKinnon exploring adventure, it may be added, the tradition further tells of how a dog accompanied the party, and emerged from the cave at some other place, but bereft of his hair. He had been in a death struggle with some monster inside and had escaped.

The dog, the same dog presumably, went into an Argyllshire cave with a piper. There are many large caves on the Kintyre coast, one of the biggest being at Keill. This cave was long the resort of smugglers, and was said to possess a subterranean passage extending six miles from the mouth of the cave to the hill of Kilellan. It was haunted, and whoseover would penetrate beyond a certain distance would never again be heard of (a very convenient tradition for smugglers). A piper, however, made up his mind to explore its inmost recesses, and, accompanied by his dog, a little terrier, he set out on the expedition, while his friends watched and listened at the cavern's mouth. The piper went in boldly, blowing his pipes till the cave resounded. His friends heard his music becoming gradually fainter and fainter until all at once, when, as they supposed, he had passed the fatal boundary, his pipes were heard to give an unearthly and tremendous skirl, while an eildrich laugh re-echoed through the cave. The terrier shortly after came running out, but without his skin. In process of time he obtained a fresh skin, but he never tried to bark after that adventure. As for the piper, his fate was purely a matter of conjecture, but he is supposed to have stumbled in the subterranean passage, for about five miles from the cavern's mouth there was a farm house, and underneath its hearthstone the piper was, in years after, often heard playing his favourite tune.

Then there is the tale of the ghostly piper of Dunderave. At certain times his music was heard issuing from a cavern which faced the sea, and into the recesses of which the waves swept. On winter nights the sounds that came from that cavern were wild and unaccountable, and often the fishermen in the vicinity were startled by fierce, bloodcurdling yells, especially in the early morning. When the tide went out, the children of the village, unaware of its terrible mystery, strayed near the yawning cavern, and occasionally sad hearts were made by the disappearance of the little ones who wandered too far in. The legend of Dunderave was that the seventh son of the seventh son of a MacGregor, who would play the gathering of his clan in the cavern, would scatter for ever the evil spirits who frequented it. A piper, who thought he had the necessary qualifications, was got, and he had the courage to play in the cavern of Dunderave. Whether he played the gathering of his clan satisfactorily or not could never be known, but certainly he never came out of the cave, the mouth of which fell in after him, blocking up the cavern for ever. No more children were lost, but ever after there could be heard by anyone standing over the cavern, the faint music of MacGregor's pipes.

A slight variation of the cave stories are the stories of underground passages. There is, for instance, the passage that is supposed to exist between Edinburgh Castle and Holyrood Palace. The piper went in at the Castle end, intending to play all the way to Holyrood. His pipes were heard as far as the Tron Church, but then the music ceased. It did not start again, and the piper was never more heard of.

A similar legend is referred to by Hugh MacDonald in his ramble, *Rutherglen and Cathkin*. It is to the effect that Glasgow Cathedral was build by the "wee pechs (Picts) who had their domicile in Rutherglen." Instead, however, of making their journeys overland, they dug an underground passage, through which they came and went. Even in MacDonald's youth , those who doubted this story were silenced and awed by the solemn assurance that a Highland piper, to put down the sceptics, had volunteered to explore the dark road. He was accompanied by his dog, and he entered playing a cheery tune, as if confident of a successful result. But "he was never seen or heard tell o' again." Only the sound of his pipes was heard as he passed underneath Dalmarnock, playing in a mournful key, which suggested the words, "I doot, I doot, I'll never get oot." Another version tells, however, that his poor dog returned, but without its skin. According to a Glasgow ballad, it was a dominie who ventured to explore the secret path. He encountered the Deil and other "friends," who blew him up through the waters of the Clyde, and the point at which he emerged became known as "The Dominie's Hole."

HUMOUR OF THE PIPES

A wandered Celt found himself laid up in an hospital in America with a disease which fairly puzzled the physicians. They did not know what to do with their patient, for he seemed to be sinking into the grave for no reason whatever. They held a consultation, and decided as a last resource to try music, preferably bagpipe music, as the patient was a Scotsman. So every night for a fortnight a piper played in the lobbies of the hospital, and gradually the Celt began to revive. At the fortnight's end he was well enough to be discharged, but - and this was the worst feature of the case - *all the other patients had died.*

Once, I remember, that story hailed from the Crimea and referred to a dying soldier of Sir Colin Campbell's, who was cured by the pipes in one hour. The music was, however, the death of forty-one of his comrades. The exact number killed varies from time to time, but that is a small matter. The incident is still the same.

The next also shows the wonderful powers of pipe music. Music, apparently, hath charms to soothe the savage *beast.* A Scotsman, a piper of course, lost his way on an American prairie, and was overtaken by a bear. To appease the brute Sandy threw it his modest lunch, the only food he had to keep him alive until he found shelter. But Bruin was not satisfied, and threatened to dine off Sandy himself, whereupon the piper thought he would play a farewell lament before quitting the world. So he struck up "Lochaber no more." No sooner, however, did the big drone give its first squeal than the bear stood stock still, then turned and fled precipitously. Then Sandy exclaimed -

"If she had known she was so fond of ta music, she could have had ta pipes before ta supper."

On its last round that story had reached Siberia, and the Celt, who was hungry, was pursued by a pack of wolves who "fled with hideous howls" when the slogan of the clan was heard.

The next illustrates the Highlander's propensity towards whisky drinking, and it rarely varies to any great extent. A Highland laird, being unable to maintain a permanent piper, employed a local musician occasionally when he had a party. Donald was once overlooked as to his usual dram before commencing to play, and in revenge he gave very bad music, which caused the laird to remonstrate with him and ask the cause. "It's the bag," said Donald; "she pe ferry, ferry hard." "And what will soften it?" asked his employer. "Och, just whusky." Accordingly the butler was sent for a tumblerful which Donald quickly drank. "You rascal," said the laird, "did you not say it was for the bagpipes?" "Och, yess, yess," said Donald; "but she will pe a ferry peculiar pipes this. She aye likes it blawed in."

A piper was on one occasion ordered to play at a wedding near Glasgow, at which his colonel was one of the guests. The object was to take the company by surprise. The piper therefore went there secretly. He had three and a half miles to walk, as the bus which plied to and fro at that time was full of ladies. The day being exceptionally wet and, he got drenched. The first incident took place shortly after leaving the barracks in the Gallowgate, where a fairly well dressed but drunken woman unceremoniously slipped her arm inside his and said – "I am going where you are going." She vowed she knew him and all the pipers, as well as all the officers, and the colonel in particular - in fact, she knew the whole regiment. While making these declarations she clung tenaciously to the piper, and nothing would shake her off. A motley crowd gathered round them, and, to make matters worse, no policeman was in sight. A gentleman, however, opportunely came to the rescue, and extricated the piper from his predicament by inviting him into a shop and letting him out by a side door into another street. In due course the piper arrived at the mansion house where he was to play. He first made for the kitchen, in order to be out of the way and to have his clothes and appointments dried and replenished. Here he was accosted by a head official, a woman, who wished to know what he was doing there and what he wanted. The piper replied that he was sent there.

"Who sent you, and what for?" she asked.

He replied - "Colonel - - -."

"And who is he?" she next asked.

"He is my colonel."

"Well," she replied, snappishly, "I don't know him and never heard anything about you."

The piper, however, entered the kitchen, and made for the fire. It so happened that the head cook - a stout, portly, good-natured woman - was a native of Tobermory. She took the drenched man in hand, and when she discovered he could speak Gaelic, they became the best of friends. He got himself so much into her favour that she undertook to dry his coat and polish all his accoutrements. In course of time he got brightened up and ready for any call. He had to ignore all the time the repelling looks and nasty hints of the head official referred to, who would have nothing to do with him, and whose dignity was evidently hurt at his presence there without her being consulted. At two in the morning he was sent for by the mistress of the house - a fine specimen of the old Scottish lady - who led him to a door which communicated with the ball-room, and, without more ado, she gave him the following instructions:-

"You'll just blow up your bags and you will play in there" - pointing to the door " and John will show you where to go to ."

The piper struck up the "Cock of the North" very suddenly, to the surprise of everyone. When he entered the room he nearly fell, the floor was so smooth. Next, his big drone touched the chandeliers, under which were standing three or four ladies with the usual long trains to their dresses. He naturally became somewhat embarrassed, for he had to watch his tune, to watch his feet, to watch the chandelier, as well as to avoid the ladies' dresses, and at the same time to watch "John", who ultimately led him into the recesses of a window, where he played the "Highland Scottische" and "Reel of Tulloch." This done, it was part of his programme to play "The Campbells are coming," and make his exit by the door through which he entered. There were, unfortunately for him, too many doors, and, as "John" had left, he was again perplexed. He, however, made for, as he thought, the proper door, under the same difficulties as he experienced on his entrance; but, instead of getting out, he was landed in a pantry where there were two young women busily engaged cutting up sandwiches. Here he was kept prisoner for about half an hour. Any pipers who have had the same experience will admit that is requires no little confidence and caution to discharge satisfactorily such duties under similar circumstances.

There is a story told of another piper, which does not terminate quite so happily. Piper Hugh MacL - was engaged to play at an Irish wedding. Now, Irish people are generally very kind, and on such occasions are possessed of a good supply of the "mercies." The room in which the wedding was held was rather small for dancing purposes, considering the number of guests. They therefore placed a table in the corner of the room, on the top of it a chair, and on the top of that a small flat stool, on which sat the piper. Here he blew with might and main till three o'clock in the morning, when down fell piper, pipes, and all on the floor. There were, luckily, no bones broken. Legs were broken, but they were wooden ones. After this somewhat amusing catastrophe the music ceased for the night.

Pipers were a resourceful race, if the following story is to be considered a typical one. A well-known piper was very often hard put to it for money, and many and various were the means he took to raise the wind. One day, more than usually dead-broke, he found an old mahogany leg of a table lying at the Clydeside, near Glasgow Green. He picked it up, and going to a joiner's shop in the Briggate, he hired a turning lathe for an hour or two. Being an expert maker as well as player, he soon had an imitation set of drones and a chanter turned out of the mahogany. Then he got a piece of old skin and made a bag which would not have kept in small stones, not to speak of wind, and by means of borrowing pence from acquaintances, he raised some green velvet and ribbons. After he had carefully covered and adorned his "pipes", he bored holes about an inch down the "drones," stained the "virls" black, and gravely offered the lot to a pawnbroker. He, poor man, did not know much about pipes, for he gave the piper cash on them. Then the dead-broke man repaid all his loans and went off a richer man. What the pawnbroker said when he attempted to sell the "pipes" is lost in the mists of time.

On one occasion a company of the Gordons were marching from a place called Jullunder to Fort Kangra, situated on one of the lower ranges of the Himalayas. Accompanying them was an elephant, on which were placed sick and exhausted men. After a few days' march they were deprived of music on account of the piper's feet becoming blistered, and he was relegated to the back of the elephant. On the last day's march, before entering their new station, some one suggested that in order to brighten them up the piper might be requested to play on the elephant's back at the head of the company. To this the officer assented, and accordingly the piper was handed his pipes. When he began to tune them up it was evident that the elephant had no appreciation of such sounds, for he shook his head, flapped his big ears menacingly, raised his trunk, with which he embraced the piper round the waist, and violently threw him and his pipes into a ditch as a mark of his disapproval of such music.